flowers IN THE *sky*

DISCARD

flowers

IN

THE

sky

LYNN JOSEPH

HARPER TEEN
An Imprint of HarperCollins*Publishers*

Page 232 poem excerpt from *Breeze Through Bamboo*, by Ema Saiko, translated by Hiroaki Sato. Copyright © 1997 Columbia University Press. Reprinted with permission of the publisher.

HarperTeen is an imprint of HarperCollins Publishers.

Flowers in the Sky

Library of Congress Cataloging-in-Publication Data
Joseph, Lynn.
  Flowers in the sky / Lynn Joseph. — 1st ed.
    p.   cm.
  Summary: "Fifteen-year-old Nina immigrates from the Dominican Republic
to New York to live with her older brother and must reconcile the realities of
Washington Heights with the dreams of the U.S. her mami envisioned for
her"— Provided by publisher.
  ISBN 978-0-06-029794-7 (hardcover bdg.)
  [1. Immigrants—Fiction.   2. Brothers and sisters—Fiction.
3. Dominican Americans—Fiction.   4. Coming of age—Fiction. 5.
Love—Fiction.   6. New York (N.Y.)—Fiction.   7. Dominican Republic—
Fiction.]   I. Title.
PZ7.J77935Flo 2013   2012038122
[Fic]—dc23

Typography by Erin Fitzsimmons
13 14 15 16 17 LP/RRDH 10 9 8 7 6 5 4 3 2 1

First Edition

For Jared Scott, who keeps me laughing,
and for Brandt Scott, who makes it all real.
I am thrilled to be your mother.

I

JUST ABOUT EVERYONE FROM my country, República Dominicana, dreams of moving to New York City, except for me. I did not want to leave my seaside home in Samana on the north coast where the humpback whales come every winter and fill Samana Bay with miracles and tourists.

But Mami kept insisting.

"Neuva York is better for you, *mi amor*," she said matter-of-factly as she rearranged items on the shelves of our little grocery store.

I knew that to Mami, better meant richer. The people of Samana were always talking about the rich gringos and gringas who lived in Neuva York. I listened to the men sitting and playing dominoes under the leafy mango tree next to our store. As I brought them Presidente beer or bags of peanuts, I heard them talking and sounding angry as they pounded the domino table and let loose about how our country's leaders steal the money from the people to build big houses and buy fancy Jeeps.

Now, everyone was also talking about our brand-new president. They say he will bring better teachers, computers, and, most of all, regular electricity. We had spent too many years in darkness because the electricity was always shutting off and stopping our clocks, our refrigerators, and in some cases, our dreams.

"He's going to open our little airport and we'll have lots of tourists," they say.

"He's going to finish that ridiculous bridge we have to nowhere," say others, pointing across the bay to our unfinished arched bridge that connects nothing.

But always the conversation came back to the rich relatives they had in Neuva York, who would send them money by Western Union or MoneyGram.

As I sat on a stool and watched Mami walk up and down the two narrow aisles of our tiny store, rearranging cans on the shelf, plumping up bread, writing down how many Pepsi-Colas we needed to order from Puerto Plata, I asked her again, "But why should I go to Neuva York?"

Mami wiped the beads of perspiration running down her face although the fan was on full blast. She looked over at me and shook her head. I knew that look. She was thinking I was strange because I didn't want to go where anyone who wants to can be rich and happy. That's what Mami had been saying for years.

And of course, Darrio was there. My brother, Darrio, whom I hardly knew because he left when I was six years old. I had only spoken to him on the telephone since then.

Now that I was fifteen, Darrio was twenty-eight and could take care of me. At least that's what Mami said. "I told you, *chica*, you will lead a better life there. Good schools, *mucho* opportunities." She rubbed her thumb and forefinger together—the universal sign for making money. She walked over to me and lifted my chin with her dusty hand. "You will meet a handsome prince, *mi amor*, a rich baseball player who will marry you and take care of your mami as she gets old and can't bend down to reach the cans on the bottom shelves."

I laughed. "No, Mami, I hate baseball." *And probably baseball players, too,* I thought.

Mami let out a big sigh. "I know. But as pretty as you are, one will marry you right away, and you will be a millionaire and come back to build your mami a solid concrete house."

A concrete house was Mami's dream. With two levels and a yard. Me, I liked our small, pink, wooden house with my garden of roses and a view of the sea. Every morning from January to March, I would peek through the flowers and shrubs to catch a glimpse of the whales frolicking in Samana Bay. If I saw any, I knew it would be a great day, because the tourists would be happy for spotting the whales and they would buy many flowers from me.

While Mami had her grocery store, I had my flowers. It started with the garden Darrio and I planted when I could barely walk. I don't know how the seeds talk to me, but I hear them. My flowers grew bigger and brighter than anyone else's in Samana. Even my roses flourished and they were difficult to grow on a tropical island. I grew roses of every color—pink, red, yellow and even a deep purple. I planted hibiscus that produced three different shades of pink flowers. Everyone in Samana called me the "flower girl." And I did not mind one bit because that was who I was, Nina Perez—the flower girl.

2

IF I KNEW ANYTHING about New York City, it was that I could not be the flower girl there. Darrio said he lived in a big building on a busy street, and there were no gardens anywhere. But there were other things that I would miss about my life in Samana, too. Like Sundays on the *malecón* with Mami.

The *malecón* is the long sidewalk that borders the edge of Samana Bay. I loved to walk with Mami, holding her big, rough hand, feeling the cool sea breeze slide over my skin, and eating *empanadas* and *quipes* from the mobile vendor. Afterward, we would drink sweet, pink sodas that matched the frills on my Sunday dress.

On Sundays, Mami and I painted bright colors on our toes and slid on sandals with small heels for our stroll on the *malecón*. First, we took a *motoconcho* there just so we wouldn't arrive hot and sweaty. The *motoconcho* in Samana is a motorcycle that has a carriage attached to the back of it for customers to ride in. The carriages are painted in all kinds of island scenes like a cool, blue ocean, or a hot, steamy jungle, or a beautiful, starry night.

Once we got to the *malecón*, Mami and I had a system. We began walking at Alfredo's Gas Station, and we stopped outside King's Department Store to buy our *empanadas* or *quipes*. Then we would walk and eat the meat pies. Finally, when we reached the *supermercado*, we would buy our sodas to sip on as we strolled slowly back down the *malecón*.

Mami and I sang along to romantic *bachatas* blaring from the stereo speakers of the tricked-out cars parked along the way. Young men with their sparkling dark eyes and quick smiles leaned on the cars, waiting for Mami to look away so they could wink at me. I smiled at them but looked down at the sidewalk quickly so that Mami would not see me and accuse me of flirting.

Sunday was also the day to see our friends strolling

along with their families. We waved *hola*, exchanged kisses on each other's cheeks, and stopped to listen to the stories of the week.

Someone usually had a fantastic tale to tell about a trip to the capital or a cousin who won the lottery. One story spun into another until the sky began changing to purple velvet, and Mami said it was time to go home. Sundays were definitely the best—like standing at the edge of the sea on a hot day and closing your eyes knowing how cool and fresh the sea would feel when it kissed your feet.

If Sunday was the cool, blue sea, then Saturday was the hot, white sand that you wished you could fly over. On Saturday mornings, I went with Mami to the Western Union office to pick up money from Darrio. Mami would stand at the window, tapping her fingers nervously on the counter until she had the pesos in her hand. Then she would swiftly count the bills, her mouth moving silently in time to her hands. As the money flew through her fingers, a smile would grow on her face. I always felt uncomfortable watching her, as if she were doing something wrong but I didn't know what.

After Mami finished counting the money, she would make the sign of the cross as if she were in church and kiss her fingers to the sky. *"Gracias, gracias,"* she said to the clouds as if the money had fallen straight from heaven to the Samana Western Union, instead of coming from my hardworking brother's pocket.

People walking by would say, "I wish I had a smart, rich son in Neuva York to send me money, too. You are very lucky, Señora Perez."

Mami would smile and say, *"Sí, sí."*

And she would start spending right away. Items for the grocery store, rum from the rum shop, and then we would both go to the beauty salon and sit under hot dryers to get our curly, dark hair straight, smooth, and silky. Finally, when all of that was done, it was my night to cook dinner. I boiled rice and stewed red beans, fried up some *plátanos* and crispy chicken for Mami and her friends while they played bingo for money and drank rum and cokes.

I fetched fresh drinks and plates of food, collected dirty glasses, and washed the dishes all before ten o'clock. Then, while Mami and her friends argued over what bingo number had been called, I stepped outside to listen to DJ Ronny play a mix of new merengues and salsa on the radio. This was finally my time alone. I danced between the rosebushes pretending I was dancing with the rich, handsome young man who Mami said would marry me one day. I didn't have a face pictured yet, but I knew he would make Mami happy. I only hoped that I would fall in love with him and that he would love me back just like in the books I got from the hotels when I dropped off my flowers for the guests. Reading in English was slow but it was good practice, and sometimes I would read all night to get to the part where the heroine finally kisses her true love. Mami said true love was nonsense and that I should focus on "real" love instead.

During the week, I tended my garden early. Even though I could see the road from my garden, I always felt sheltered inside a cocoon of blossoms and thick foliage. I had started growing a new kind of sunflower that I hoped would win a prize at our Dia de Santa Bárbara festival. I wished I could sit all day and watch my sunflowers turn their gold-and-black faces to the sun, following it like sun worshippers. But I couldn't stay long because I had to race down the hill to school.

3

SCHOOL WAS PROBABLY THE only thing I wouldn't miss if I had to go to Neuva York. My best friends, Mirabel and Eva, didn't go to school with me anymore, so I had to walk by myself no matter what the weather was like—rainy or sunny, hazy or humid. I did not have them to laugh with, or tease about which boys Eva liked, or whisper about the magical paintings by the foreign artists who came to Samana to paint the bay and the whales and our town.

I had read almost every single book in our tiny school library, and I couldn't bring my books from the hotels to school. So I had nothing to read while the teacher explained the same thing over and over. I looked out the window and wished for something magical to happen. Maybe a strange new boy might walk in and sit next to me, smiling a slow, sweet smile. There was no boy in town I liked as yet. But all of the boys seemed to be smiling at me these days and Mami said it was because I now had the "scent of a woman," whatever that meant. She called all of the boys "*tigueritos*," which meant they were bad boys! How did she know that?

The best part of school was walking home in the afternoons, when I could stop and watch the artists on the *malecón*. They were from France and Germany, Canada and Italy, from so many different countries, but many spoke Spanish and would talk to me. We had a lot of paintings by Dominican and Haitian artists for sale in the souvenir shops, but I never saw any of them painting outside. These foreign artists wore smocks splashed with colors and had paintbrushes twisted into their hair or stuck behind their ears. They looked so happy that I wondered if maybe I would like to be a painter, too.

One young woman painted the same thing over and over—groves of swaying coconut trees that looked like policemen with green-feathered caps guarding the beach.

Her brush flew over the canvas mixing dark greens and light olives together. From the expression on her face, I could tell she wasn't happy with her painting, but I thought it was beautiful and I told her so.

She shook her head fiercely. "No, it isn't. I have to get it just right."

I didn't tell her, but I thought that only God could get it just right. Hers would just be a copy. But I kept my mouth shut because maybe I was wrong. Maybe there was something about art that I didn't understand. The same way I didn't understand Mami and her desire for money and a concrete house. The look on the artist's face was the same look Mami got sometimes. Not desperate, but straining—like an animal on a leash trying to reach something far away.

Once in a while, I'd see a painting that made my heart flutter wildly. I'd sit on the low stone ledge staring at it, which Mami said was pure foolishness. But I'd get lost in the colors and light and feel like I was being pulled right into the canvas. It was almost as if the paintings had a secret to reveal, and I had to figure it out. When that happened, the artist, whoever it was, would leave the painting right there for me to enjoy, and sometimes he or she would ask me, "What do you see?"

And once, just once, I was able to reply, "I see everything."

So, that was my life in Samana. The life Mami wanted me to leave behind to go to the big, glittering city of Neuva York. Mami could not understand that I already had plenty of glitter right at my feet in Samana. And although she harped on New York, Mami never did anything about it, until the day she saw me sitting too close to a man. It was then that everything changed.

4

MIRABEL, EVA, AND I were the same age and had grown up knowing we would be friends for life. We built a fort in the mango tree in Eva's backyard when we were eight years old and hid there during a hurricane until our parents found us and smacked us for being so foolish. We went to school together, sewed Sunday dresses, painted our faces at *carnaval*, and danced merengue and salsa, teaching each other new moves and spins.

Then, we turned twelve. It was Eva's body that changed first. She grew breasts that made men stop and stare and whistle at her. Then Mirabel's body sprang right up like a sleek mermaid. Last of all, when I was finally fourteen, my body caught up with theirs, and I had breasts and a waist and hips so that Mami said I must never, no matter what, ever be alone with a boy. I had to take Mami or Eva or Mirabel with me just to go to the *colmado* to buy bread because Javier was at the counter and he waited to flirt with girls like me, Mami said.

Another big change happened at fourteen. Eva and Mirabel stopped going to school with me. They had decided to start their own business. At least until they found young men to marry and have babies with, they said. Every day, on my way to school, Eva and Mirabel waved to me as they set up a table under a mango tree to sell their toe rings and dreams. That's what the sign said. Mirabel with her long, black hair and quick smile was in charge of getting customers, and it was she who waved people over to the "shop." Eva was heavier with a sweet smile and the prettiest face in Samana. She could pick out the perfect ring for anyone. Together, they were a hit with the tourists, and I thought they were exciting for leaving school and working all day.

But as time went by, people began talking about Mirabel and Eva, saying they were flirting too much with the German tourists and that the dreams they were selling were sex. I never saw anything unusual, but I heard stories about my friends eating in fancy restaurants with men late at night.

"*Putas*," people said, and shook their heads sadly. I ignored them because I knew how Dominicans liked to gossip. But then it happened. Without any warning, my perfect world disappeared. Mami mistook me for a *puta*.

I was walking home from school one day, and Mirabel and Eva called me over.

"Nina," they shouted, "come sit with us."

I was supposed to change my clothes and go straight-away to help Mami in the grocery store. But the sun was shining through the mango tree leaves, and Mirabel was twirling Eva to my favorite merengue playing on their CD player, and they were laughing and singing, so I stopped. I wanted some of that magic, too.

I walked over to them and sat in one of their chairs at the table full of silver toe rings and coral anklets.

"Try one on," said Mirabel, pulling off my shoe and putting my foot on her lap.

I giggled. "No, Mami would kill me if I wore a toe ring."

Eva handed Mirabel a silver ring with a tiny pink flower on top. "Perfect," laughed Mirabel, and she slipped it on my toe. "There, Nina, a present from us."

I looked down at my plain brown legs and feet, and that tiny, perfect flower on my toe was like a flag of womanhood staring me in my face. It was the true essence of me. For the first time ever, I felt a shiver of excitement about what was coming in life. It was not all about books and selling flowers and taking walks and eating pies. Something exciting would happen in my life, and that flower was the beginning.

A few moments later, two blond German men walked over, talking and laughing and calling Mirabel and Eva by name. I stood up to leave, but Mirabel pulled me back down.

"Just a little fun," Mirabel said as she winked and waved at the men.

"Mirabel, no," I whispered as one man came and sat beside me. His hand hovered over my brown skin.

"Nice legs," he said, and I hurriedly tucked my legs under the chair.

"It's okay, Nina, we know them," said Eva.

The other German man slid into a chair next to Eva. She was sitting forward and the tops of her heavy breasts showed clearly in her white shirt.

I tried to snake away from the man's hand that hovered over my legs. He had a red beard and huge feet in brown, leather sandals. In his right hand, he dangled the keys to the Jeep parked at the curb. He smiled and swung the keys in front of my eyes. I shook my head at him.

At that very moment, I smelled Mami's lavender toilet water scent and heard the solid *clomp, clomp* of her work shoes.

"Oh, Nina, it's your mami." Eva looked at me with eyes wide open, while she quickly buttoned her shirt with one hand.

I brushed the German man's hand away from my leg and pushed the dangling keys out of my face, but it was too late. Mami was heading toward us like a thick, dark wave. The *clomp, clomp* of her heavy shoes kept time with my heart. Even from where I was sitting, I could see Mami's eyes were narrowed and her eyebrows were fanned out like wings of fury. Her eyes stared at the spot on my leg where the man's hand had been.

Mami stopped in front of us—Mirabel, Eva, and me and the two German strangers. I felt tiny pinpricks of fear creeping up my skin. It was the not knowing that I was afraid of. I had never seen her so angry.

Then, with a vicious swing of her arm, Mami reached over and grabbed me right out of my seat and into the air. I landed on my feet, but almost fell back. Mami held my arm tightly next to her body, and my gray school skirt was raised high, showing my bare legs to all on the *malecón*.

I tried to pull down my skirt, but Mami sneered, "Don't bother now." She shook me hard.

"Stop, Mami," I cried. "Stop."

"This girl is not a *puta*," Mami spat. She shook me like a tree branch at the German men. Then she glared at Mirabel and Eva.

Mirabel gasped. Eva was crying. The men were staring at us, probably not understanding a word of Mami's scornful Spanish. Then they stood up and left, talking their deep-throated language.

Mami let go of my arm, but not before she smacked me. "You are not a *puta*," she said, her teeth clenched tightly.

I was so ashamed that I couldn't even say good-bye to Eva and Mirabel as I followed Mami down the *malecón* toward home. The next week, Mami spent a lot of time talking on the telephone to Darrio in New York.

"I'm sending you to a better life," Mami told me. "You will live with your brother, and he'll make sure you meet the right men and get married to a rich Yankee."

I didn't want to go to New York and leave Samana and my flowers and my friends and the Sunday walks. But it was no use telling Mami anything. She was determined.

I didn't know how Mami was planning to get me to New York since I had no visa and there wasn't a soul at the US Embassy about to grant a visa to a teenage Dominican girl with no money, no land, and no connections. Mami called Darrio on the phone and complained and cried until he broke down and agreed to buy me a visa. That was my first true sin. Leaving my country on a lie.

Some would argue that it does not count as a sin since it was a law we were breaking and not a moral commandment like thou shalt not steal or kill. Bit it didn't matter how you classified it, I knew that I was going to have to pretend to be something I wasn't in order to travel to a new world. Within days I had a passport and a visa stamped inside that said I could travel to the United States. I was on my way.

Mami packed me up, and we took a bus to the Puerto Plata airport. The whole way there, Mami kept saying that this was best for me. This would be my grand opportunity. I did not believe her, but Mami was so insistent that I was going to a better life in New York that I just bent my head and tried not to cry as the green coconut trees with their feathered caps flew past the bus window.

5

ON THE FLIGHT TO New York, my first time on a plane, my first time away from Mami, I was finally free to cry. But nothing came out. No tears. No sobs. Nothing. It was as if my feelings were strangled tightly inside my chest. I leaned my forehead against the plastic window and watched as the green mountains of my beloved island slipped away far below. I sat very still, blocking out the excited chatter of the passengers around me. I was leaving my country for all the wrong reasons. Like being sentenced for a crime I never committed. How long would it be before I saw Samana again? Or the blossoming of my new ginger lilies? And what about my sunflowers? As these thoughts swirled through my head, I closed my eyes, feeling the heat of the bright sun shining on me through my little plastic window. I forgot about everyone around me and drifted into my thoughts.

My brother, Darrio! When was the last time I saw him? What would he be like now after ten years living in Neuva York? For the first time since this whole fiasco with Mami, I felt a tiny ray of hope. It was because of my last memory of my brother. I was five years old, and Darrio was eighteen and still living in Samana. It was Dia de Santa Bárbara, and the village was preparing for the annual Fiesta. Each Dominican town has its own saint who guards it and watches over its inhabitants. And each town has its own saint's day.

I was in the garden, already dressed up and ready to go into town with Mami and Darrio for the big celebration.

"Nina! Nina!" Mami called me.

I was busy patting down the soil around Darrio's desert rosebushes. He had planted them the year before. I remember Darrio coming home with cuttings from the gardens of the fancy homes where he worked as a gardener. I had sat on an overturned bucket and watched him plant them in our garden, his hands large and firm as he showed me how to make sure they got just enough dirt and light and water. Already the garden was blooming with flowers of every color.

On the day of the fiesta, I heard Mami calling but I wanted to finish with the shrubs first. Finally, I got up off the ground, dusted off my knees, and went running straight to the yard, where the pickup truck was parked. Mami was standing there in her party dress.

"Look at you, Nina!" she cried.

I looked down. My knees were black with dirt, and a smudge lingered on the hem of my dress. Before Mami could say another word, Darrio came strolling out of the house, saying calmly, "Hush, Mami, hush. It's okay, she doesn't look so bad."

Darrio reached down and swung me up into his strong arms and rested me on his hip. He was smiling and handsome, and his black eyes glittered beneath a heavy shadow of lashes that touched his face. I stroked his long, black eyelashes very gently. They were softer than anything I knew.

Darrio dusted off my knees with one hand while he held me up with the other.

"You ready to dance with your big brother, Nina?"

I nodded my head and my ponytail swung back and forth. "Sí."

We got into the truck and headed down the hill into town. As we got closer, the merengue music vibrated through me, and I tapped my feet on the center console, where I sat between Mami and Darrio.

Then, we rounded the last corner, and there was the town. It was laid out like a giant birthday cake with bright-colored flags waving in the breeze, festive balloons bobbing high above, and paintings on easels lined up for sale, their colors shimmering in the brilliant sunlight. I knew exactly where I wanted to go first.

As soon as Darrio parked the truck, I grabbed his hand. "Come on, I want to go see the paintings."

"*Mi amor*, what about a dance first?" Darrio swung his hips in time to the loud merengue music coming from the stage in the center of town.

A group of girls walked by and waved at Darrio. "Save us a dance," one of them cooed and winked at Darrio.

I rolled my eyes. Girls were always asking Darrio to dance with them. That could wait.

"But I want to see the paintings."

Darrio looked over at the sidewalk where the artists hovered in front of their crafts. "Okay," he agreed. "But you have to promise me the first dance as soon as we finish looking."

I nodded fast and pulled his hand. Darrio told Mami we would meet her next to the ancient ceiba tree, and my brother and I walked off hand in hand.

We weaved in and out of people, making our way along the sidewalk. The smell of oil paints and sweat filled my senses.

"Look at this one, Darrio." I peeked between the bodies blocking our view.

"I'll be able to see it when they move. But what is it a painting of?"

"It looks like a thousand flowers."

"That must be a lot of colors."

I nodded. "Just like our garden."

"What kind of blossoms, *mi amor*?"

At that moment, the man in front of me moved, and I saw clearly what I had only glimpsed before: a world of radiant colors, lighting up the canvas, exactly like our garden at home.

"Darrio!" I shouted. "It's our garden."

"Really? Someone painted our garden?"

Then the person in front of Darrio moved, too, and Darrio squeezed my hand. "I think you're right, Nina."

There before us were our red jasmines and yellow frangipanis and the blood-red blossoms of our geiger tree.

They looked so alive. From the coral jumby-bead bush we planted last Christmas to the trumpet-shaped yellow flowers of our esperanza shrubs trailing over the fence, this magnificent painting had it all.

"Look at all the morning glories, Darrio! And our angel's trumpet tree."

"I see them." Darrio's voice sounded like it was coming from far away. "I see it all, *princessa*."

The artist stood next to the easel displaying the painting.

"I know you," I said to her. I meant to say I knew her painting.

She smiled at me. "I know you, too."

Darrio grinned and introduced himself. The artist had a funny accent, and she wore a loose sundress with pockets that had the tops of paintbrushes peeking out.

"That's our garden." I pointed to her largest painting.

She looked surprised. "I saw it one day as I was walking in the hills. It was so beautiful that I walked past it every day as I exercised. Pretty soon I felt as if I knew every tree and flower in it."

I knew every tree and flower in our garden, too. As if they were my friends.

"My brother planted it all."

Darrio cleared his throat. "*We* planted it," he corrected.

The girl looked at my brother, and her eyes glowed. "It's magnificent." Then she bent down and reached into a box on the ground. She rooted around for a minute and pulled out a square, flat object wrapped in linen. "I know you have the garden, so you don't need this, but it would be my pleasure if you accepted this small painting from me."

A painting of our very own. We could never afford any of the beautiful paintings. But this was a gift.

Darrio unwrapped the cloth, and there was a miniature version of the same large painting of our garden.

"I always do small paintings first, just to see what it would look like."

"Thank you," said Darrio. "We don't know any artists. It's a gift we will treasure."

"Thank *you*," said the girl. "You created something that is so beautiful I had to paint it."

Darrio and I stood close together looking at the painting. "Now we will never forget it," he whispered to me.

"Of course we won't forget it. We'll have our garden forever, won't we?"

Darrio didn't answer me, but I did not care. Some things you know are true, even if the grown-ups don't agree. The rest of the fiesta day was a blur. Darrio and I put the painting in the truck and went to find Mami. She was standing next to the ceiba tree as promised.

"I have beef *empanadas* for everybody." She handed out the meat pies to Darrio and me.

Darrio bought us drinks from a vendor, and we stood under the shade of the tree, eating and watching the dancers twirling around to the music. A bold *chica* came by and asked Darrio to dance. He shook his head no.

"I promised someone else first."

The girl giggled. "Okay, but don't forget me." She walked off, wiggling in her tight dress and swinging her highlighted hair.

"I'm never going to look like that," I said beneath my breath.

But Darrio heard me. "You'd better not, *princessa*. I will never dance with you again."

We both laughed, and Mami looked at us confused as if she had no idea what we were talking about. When the next song started, Darrio bowed in front of me like a handsome knight. "My dance, *mi amor?*"

Darrio put my feet on top of his, and we swirled off into the giddiness of the music. When the song ended, Darrio took me back to Mami, but before he could let go of my hand, another *chica* was approaching him.

Mami frowned. "These girls today."

I knew Mami didn't like the girls who circled Darrio like a school of fish. She shook her head. "Your brother is too popular for his own good."

I wondered what she meant. Being popular sounded like a bad thing. But when I looked over at Darrio's laughing face, I saw nothing but happiness. We stayed until the last drumbeat. Then we gathered up our small purchases and my balloon and headed to the pickup truck for the drive up into the hills of Samana.

Two weeks later, Darrio had to leave Samana and go to find work in Neuva York. I begged Mami not to let him go. But Mami just sat at the table with a stack of papers in front of her and a look on her face that meant she was missing my father. I never knew Papi. He had died when I was a baby. Darrio used to tell me funny stories about Papi to help me remember him. But I only remembered Darrio's stories.

Now, Mami's face was like flat stone, and her hands lay

heavily on the papers in front of her.

Mami said solemnly. "Darrio's the man of the house now."

Darrio took me in his arms and carried me outside. The sea breeze blew my hair all about and into my eyes, which made them tear up. Darrio gathered my hair into one of his hands. "*Princessa*, don't cry."

I sniffled into his shirt. "But I don't want you to go."

He patted my head. I touched his velvet eyelashes softly. They were wet, just like mine.

While Darrio waited for one of his friends to drive him to the airport in Puerto Plata, he circled our garden a few times and touched the leaves of the calabash tree. We heard the honks of the car outside, and Darrio picked up his bag to walk out the door. I ran after him with the small painting of our garden. I didn't say a word. I shoved it at him and ran out the back door. I went straight to our garden and sat down under the bushes, hiding from Mami. I refused to go inside even after Mami stopped calling my name.

6

MOVING STEPS. YOU HAVE to jump on fast or you will get left behind, or worse, eaten by the giant metal snake they call an escalator. My first stop in New York's John F. Kennedy Airport was the immigration line. I stood behind a tangle of other Dominicans, their carry-on bags strewn haphazardly, making the line rocky and dangerous. In their hands they clutched passports, ready to show their legal status to be in the United States. I slid my passport into the pocket of my jeans, trying to stop my heart from racing up into my throat. I was worried that an immigration official with a big, black gun on his hip would yank me out of line and take me to an interrogation room. I had heard about it from others who had tried to enter this sacred country and never made it past the airport.

It was my turn, and I approached with a huge knot tying my tongue. I could barely answer the questions posed in Spanish. Where would I be staying? How long? With whom? What were my plans while here? All questions that Mami had rehearsed with me. My answers made my knees shake.

Finally, the officer was satisfied, and he stamped my passport. "Welcome to the United States."

"Thank you," I said in perfect English. He looked at me with surprise. I hurried off, stuffing my passport into my pocket and dragging my bag behind me.

I exited the customs area and tumbled into hordes of people. Pandemonium everywhere. People screeched in delight, hugging family and lovers. Some waved signs that read *Welcome Home*. I struggled through, not knowing where to look. I kept my eyes straight ahead, pushing aside luggage and boxes and wondering if anyone would claim me, too.

That's when I saw the bouquet of bright flowers— orange lilies, pink roses, yellow carnations and posies. I focused on the flowers and walked toward them like they were beacons of light. A brown hand came into focus. It grasped the flowers carefully, just the way I remembered it.

I looked up and saw my big brother—handsome and strong and silent. But he was not looking at me. He was staring at the door from which I had just exited.

"Darrio?"

My brother looked down at me with a stranger's eyes. Then, suddenly, a smile broke over his face.

"Ni-na? That can't be you?" He laughed and threw his arms around me. Then he stepped back and looked me up and down, reaching out and rumpling my hair. His eyes crinkled in the corners. I stared at the long, black eyelashes that fluttered closed for a second as if he couldn't believe I was really there and he had to blink to make sure it was true.

It was Darrio, but he smelled different. Like something dried and closed up. He handed me the bouquet of flowers, and I hugged it close. It was the only thing in this new world that was familiar.

"Let's go home." Darrio reached for my hand and my bag.

We got on a subway—the A train, Darrio called it. It

had a big, glowing blue A on the front that flashed by as it flew into the subway station. Although we got on at the first stop, the seats were grabbed immediately by hundreds of people with their bags, parcels, and suitcases. Darrio showed me how to hold on to a metal pole, and he tried to stay close to me, as the subway swayed side to side and jolted to a stop. Every time the doors opened, more people got on, and Darrio and I soon got separated. I thought the windows would burst open from the pressure of so many people. The worst part was when they raised their arms over my head to reach a higher part of the metal pole. I was forced to inhale the smell of their underarms, which stank like old rum bottles.

I clutched my flowers tighter, watching the blooms wilt and fade, crushed by the throngs of people. It was like watching something that had been so vibrant and alive a few moments ago die right in front of my eyes. They were not going to make it, not even to Darrio's home.

Just when I thought I couldn't last another minute, either, and that I would faint right there beneath all those feet and get trampled to death, the people cleared out, and Darrio pulled me into a seat. I was sweating and dizzy.

I looked at Darrio, who smiled at me and squeezed my hand. "It's okay, Nina. We're almost there."

I tried to smile back, but I couldn't move one muscle in my face. It would get better as soon as we reached Darrio's home. It had to. We'd drink some sweet café con leche and feel better. I tried to listen as Darrio told me about New York, but I didn't comprehend a word of it. Finally, Darrio stood up and began gathering my bags. "Time to go, *princessa*."

I followed him up and out into the bright sunshine of a hot summer evening. People pushed past me as they hurried toward the subway steps behind us. We were standing on a concrete island surrounded on three sides by cars and buses whizzing by, blowing their horns, squealing their tires to avoid people dashing across the street toward the subway.

"Rush hour," said Darrio.

As I looked around, I wondered, *What kind of world is this?* "This is where you live?"

"Welcome to Washington Heights," he said.

It was humid, and the sidewalks smelled of burnt tar. This heat was so different from back home, where the sea breezes blew in fresh air that kissed my skin and blew my long hair into ribbons that fluttered off my neck.

Here, the black streets steamed with fire, hotter than any day in Samana. I could hear rumbles of merengue music coming from stores along the street. Tall, brown buildings loomed in the sky, with clothes streaming out of windows like colorful flags. A multitude of stores were lined up, one jumbled next to the other, selling food, clothes, the *Listin Diario* newspaper, Spanish *Cosmo* magazines, phone cards, liquor, and suitcases.

There were money shops for sending money back home, and shops with telephone booths lined up side by side to call home. There were windows filled with phone cards in bright colors offering the "best rate to República Dominicana." Cards for five dollars; ten dollars; twenty dollars in reds, blues, magentas, and yellows—it was as if the phone cards were flowers sprouting out of the store windows.

Darrio stopped outside one of the *colmados* that had signs advertising *yuca* and *plátanos*. There were words scrawled in black that I couldn't read.

He said something to the man behind the counter, and then Darrio introduced me as his *princessa* from the Island. The man nodded and shook my hand. "Welcome to America."

"You can buy food here instead of walking to the

supermercado, Nina," Darrio told me, pointing to items like coffee and milk.

I nodded, wondering where Darrio's home could possibly be.

I followed my brother out the store and up the street, dodging people everywhere. Old men playing dominoes on tables set up blocking the sidewalks, teenagers with babies in spanking-new strollers, teenagers in big pants and T-shirts so long that the hems of the shirts almost touched their sneakers. Older women sat on folding chairs, propped up against the brick walls, curlers in their hair, doing their nails. Car brakes screeched as people walked in front of cars thumping the hoods as if to say, "Thanks for not hitting me." Buses roared by and passengers ran for them, waving newspapers in the air and shouting obscenities as the buses drove off without them. I couldn't believe a bus would deliberately leave a passenger. Back home, the bus would wait forever to catch an extra fare.

I rubbed my eyes and surveyed the grimy colors. There was not one coconut tree or hibiscus flower anywhere. Instead, I saw frowns and heard cursing and felt a thickness of fear and regret permeating the air. These were my people. They were Dominicanos like me, far away from our beautiful country with its blue seas and green mountains, the loud laughter, and the carefree dancing in the streets. Did they forget about all that?

These were the same people who came back home each year exclaiming about the joys of life in New York and bestowing gifts upon every single person. These were the people who always looked so happy when they walked off the plane and grabbed a cold Presidente beer from the nearest shop and hugged their family members, telling them tales of the riches in New York.

Back home, I had heard young men declare loudly, "When I go to New York, I'm going to get rich or die." I didn't know about the getting rich part, but death was definitely here. I could feel it. I looked around and wondered why no one else could.

"Why does everyone look so angry?" I asked Darrio.

"It's just New York."

"But I thought everyone loved New York. Everybody wants to come here."

"Yes, *mi amor*, we all love New York best when we are actually back home."

It made no sense, and I wondered what was the point?

"Mami told me you were *muy inteligente*." Darrio walked into one of the big buildings that lined the street. "She said you could speak English very well, is that true?"

"Yes, I've studied English for five years."

"I know. I sent Mami extra money just for those lessons. Now you can use it here."

"Oh." Mami never told me it was Darrio who paid for my English classes. She always told me about the new shoes or beauty salon appointments she had to give up for me to go to the English school.

I followed along behind Darrio, up stairs where I smelled *tostones* and *chicharrones* frying through the closed doors. So many closed doors. I had never in my life imagined that a building could have so many doors.

Then we stopped and Darrio pushed a button impatiently. Suddenly, a loud noise, a crack, and a part of the wall opened up to reveal a black, grated box—an elevator. I had heard about them, but I had never seen one before. We got inside, and Darrio slammed the black grate closed and the box moved up. The smell inside was atrocious—like old diapers and sour milk. I closed my eyes. The smell and the feeling inside the closed box scared me. This was not the paradise I heard so much about. This was hell, pure and simple.

Finally, the box stopped and we got off and walked to a door that looked just like all the other doors. Darrio unlocked the door, and I followed him inside.

It was like waking up on Christmas morning and finding nothing under the tree. Not even a chocolate. The room was bare. As if it had been emptied of life to make room for what? Me? On closer look, I saw a card table leaning against one wall, along with metal chairs that were folded up.

"We're getting furniture, Nina, don't worry. I just never needed any before."

"That's okay," I lied.

I looked at my big brother under cover of my hair, which hung like a curtain between us. His eyes couldn't lie, even if his voice was filled with cheerfulness. I recognized a plant whose roots were so deep and tangled it could not raise itself up into the light.

Darrio showed me the kitchen, which, unlike the living room had signs of life.

He grinned at me. "My girlfriend, Marla, bought new pots for you. Mami said you were a good cook."

Mami had obviously said a lot of things to convince Darrio to send me a visa. My cooking was definitely just for survival purposes. At home, my hands and fingernails were always so dirty from the garden that Mami hardly let me touch the food.

Then Darrio showed me my room. It was tiny, but had a beautiful, white iron bed and a small dresser; on top of the dresser was a blue glass vase filled with fresh flowers.

I felt guilty for thinking negative thoughts about Darrio.

"Thank you," I whispered, and for the first time since I arrived, I reached out to hug my brother.

"Wait until you see the best part." He walked over to the window and pulled it up. There was a metal grate in front of the window that he opened. "*Mira*, look, *princessa*, just for you."

I peeked out. The ground was far below, but right outside the window was a narrow, metal landing. And a black metal ladder hung down to the next landing below.

"It's a fire escape," said Darrio.

I must have looked puzzled because he explained that since we lived so far from the ground, if ever there was a fire, we could get out safely.

"These Americans think of everything, *mi amor.*"

I looked out at the fire escape and wondered why Darrio thought it was the best part of the room. He climbed out of the room through the window and beckoned me to follow.

"I don't think so."

Darrio shrugged his shoulders. "Okay, but it's like your own private world out here, *princessa*."

I glanced at the metal grate, the ground far, far below and the brown buildings that rose like huge walls around us. I could not see how this fire escape was a private world at all. It looked scary to me.

"No, Darrio. I'd rather stay right here."

He climbed back in the window and stood in the small room awkwardly, his hands in his pockets.

I should be grateful. I knew I had the power to smile and make it all okay. But it wasn't okay. I didn't want to be here. I didn't want to go outside on a ledge high above the ground. I couldn't help but think of my other private world with its multitude of flowers.

I looked into Darrio's waiting face. "It's great," I said.

Darrio didn't say anything at all. He just turned his head and looked out the window at the street and the bustling people below. It was as if he already knew what I felt.

Once, Mami had taken me to the *campo* where she grew up and showed me her old home. The countryside had many fruit trees and grassy land for racing donkeys, but not much else. Mami had had to leave school before she had even started it, at seven years old, to make charcoal to sell for her family. I had seen the many holes in Mami's backyard, which Mami had spent her childhood filling with wood to then burn it into charcoal. Mami had showed me the empty sacks she would use to bag the charcoal and sell it to neighbors for cooking. I told myself that Mami only wanted something better for me. But better didn't have to mean lots of money. While Mami had visions of a rich husband, I wanted only to grow flowers.

Darrio left and closed the door, giving me privacy. I lay down on the tiny bed and stared at the vase of flowers on the dresser. *When will I see my home again?* I wondered. I closed my eyes and turned my head to the wall. And who would I become, now that I was not the flower girl?

7

I FELL ASLEEP WITHOUT any dinner. When I opened
my eyes again, a dim light was coming through the window and I could hear the sounds of doors opening and
closing, a teakettle whistling, trucks rumbling by, and
sirens blaring below. I shook my head to wake up. It
was real. I was here in New York City and, other than
Darrio, I didn't know anyone. Even though I was mad at
Mami, I wished she was here with me now; just to hear
her grumbling would be better than this hollow feeling
I had. I glanced around the room and shivered. I didn't
know what I was supposed to do. Usually, I jumped

straight out of bed and ran to my garden.

On the floor by my bed was my small, unopened suitcase, waiting, like me, for some kind of beginning. Darrio must have put it there last night. I didn't have many clothes for this new life, but Mami had said that Darrio would take me shopping after I arrived. Fortunately, it was May, and the air was warm and slightly sticky, so my island clothes would be fine for now.

A knock on the bedroom door interrupted my thoughts. Darrio was calling my name.

"Come in."

Darrio peeked in with a smile and a glass of juice. "I figured you might be thirsty."

I drank the juice in one gulp and wiped my mouth with the top of my T-shirt.

Darrio was pointing to the dresser drawer where there was a towel and extra sheets.

"Get ready and I will show you Washington Heights. We also have to register you for high school. There's still one month left and you might as well start right away. Plus, you can go to summer school to catch up."

"I'm going to school?" I asked.

Darrio looked surprised. "Of course."

"Oh, I thought I was supposed to get a job and work to make money."

Darrio laughed a shrill, unnatural laugh. "Over my dead body."

"Mami said I had to earn my way and pay you back for my visa."

Darrio sat down on the edge of the bed. His eyes had wrinkles in the corners that I did not remember and a shadow in them that was never there before. I couldn't adjust to this older man. I recalled Darrio in the kitchen surrounded by measuring cups of plant food, laughing and twirling me about, teasing Mami, fixing things in the house, and drinking beer with his feet up against the porch rails. The memories flashed swiftly like a movie unfolding. It stopped and I looked at the tough, stiff man in front of me. This same man was Darrio? I felt that he was and he wasn't. Like one of those optical illusions you have to stare at for a while before you can see the image.

Darrio was looking at me strangely, too, and I wondered if he also was thinking of me from long ago.

Suddenly, Darrio reached for my hand.

"*Princessa*, no matter that we haven't seen each other in a long, long time, I am your brother and you are my sister."

Darrio patted my hand awkwardly. "And that means you're going to school, and I'm going to take care of you. That's how it is."

"Okay," I said. I wanted so badly to tell Darrio that I didn't want to be here.

"And things are different here, but I promised Mami that you would meet some nice people and date a nice boy, not a *tiguerote* or a tourist."

I wondered if Darrio believed Mami's tales that I was almost a *puta*. It was so ridiculous. But I couldn't talk about that with Darrio.

"Okay," I said again, because truthfully there was nothing else left to say or do. I was here. I was in New York, and no one ever left New York to go back home to the República Dominicana unless it was for a vacation. It was unheard of. Now I knew how it felt to be rudely uprooted and replanted in the wrong soil.

Darrio and I set out a little later, after a breakfast of café con leche and boiled plantains mashed with butter and cinnamon, my secret spice that I put on everything. And just as baffling as Darrio seemed to me, the neighborhood of Washington Heights was no different.

St. Nicholas Avenue, the main thoroughfare, twisted and flowed like a river with undercurrents of subway noises and a torrent of people, shops, goods, vendors, traffic, and posters forcing us to curve and bend around them as we made our way through. No matter how I tried I could not seem to get my bearings. Like on the *malecón*, people stopped suddenly to say hello and chat, and I bumped into shoulders and legs. At the end of the block, we arrived at the *colmado* again, and this time we went all the way inside.

"Darrio, who's that?" was the first thing I heard.

The heavyset woman had gray braids that were twisted and tied on her head, and she was sitting at the cash register near the door.

"Señora Rivera, this is my little sister, Nina, from the island. She just arrived here yesterday."

I stretched out a hand to shake hers, but she stepped from behind the register and embraced me in a big, warm hug. "*Bienvenido*, Nina."

"*Gracias.*"

Señora Rivera shook her head at Darrio. "She's not so

little, *jefe*. Watch out for these sharks on the street."

Darrio smirked. "Nina is not interested in boys, Señora Rivera. She's here to go to high school and then college."

Señora Rivera nodded her head. "That's right." She wiped her hands on her stiff, black shirt and looked at me with fierce eyes, as if I would defy her.

I nodded my head to show her that I would study hard. She smiled and reached behind the counter. "Here, come see me again." She placed something in my hand before going to ring up another customer.

In my hand, Señora Rivera had placed a cluster of sweets—small *dulces* in pretty-colored papers. I looked up at Darrio and grinned. I was not used to getting candies in the middle of the week.

We left the *colmado* and continued our walk along St. Nicholas Avenue. Near the end of the next block was a barbershop, with Dominican flags fluttering from the posts by the door. Suddenly, the door flew open and reggaeton music blared out as two young men trooped onto the sidewalk talking and laughing. The shorter, stocky one called out to some girls walking by. As we approached, the stocky boy nudged the tall, lean boy in his side and whispered something to him.

The tall boy glanced up from his cell phone just as I was walking in front of him, and I found myself looking up into eyes so green and clear that the entire city seemed captured within them. The boy's gaze locked on me with such an intensity that I stumbled. Darrio reached out for me, but the boy was quicker and his hand caught me before I fell.

"*Cuidado,*" he said.

A strong blush burned up my face, and my heart did a crazy flip. I couldn't look away from his face.

Darrio finally took my hand and led me away.

"Who was that?" I blurted out. Darrio didn't answer me, and there was a frown on his face as he looked at the boys. Were these the "sharks" Señora Rivera had warned us about?

I looked down at myself to see what the green-eyed boy had seen: a girl with long, curly black hair wearing a simple cotton skirt and a flowered T-shirt, with leather sandals on her feet that were made in Samana. On my left toe, the pink flower ring winked up at me. It was comforting to have a piece of home with me at all times. I glanced back at the boys and wondered if they were like the young men at home that flirted with me when Mami was not looking. Maybe that was all it was, a little smile, a look, a flirtation that meant nothing at all. The men from my country were famous for their charm and reputations with the *muchachas*. I heard about the *hombres de la calle* all the time and how to avoid them. This was nothing new to me. Yet something felt different about this boy. I glanced back and he was standing in the middle of the sidewalk, his head cocked to one side, watching us walk away.

Unlike me, Darrio did not glance at the boys again, and instead, was busy pointing out more shops to me: the beauty salon, the shoe repair, but the most important one, he stressed, was the Envios de Valores La Nacional, the money transfer store where he went every Friday evening to send money home to Mami.

"We can call from there, too," he said. "You get one free phone call when you send money."

I nodded, knowing only too well what it was like to be at the money transfer place back home waiting for the American dollars to be changed into pesos.

Darrio also took me to the *farmacia*, where I could buy the personal items I needed. Next door to the *farmacia* was a restaurant with a neon sign: THE LATIN STAR. Yellow signs in the windows advertised the daily specials.

"The *sancocho* is *delicioso* here," said Darrio. "We can come here sometimes if you want." I nodded, remembering the smell of Mami's *sancocho*. Mami and I never went to restaurants.

Outside the Latin Star stood three girls a little older than me. They were smoking cigarettes and talking loudly. Their lipstick mouths were a bright ruby red, and their nails were like decorated missiles flicking ashes across the sidewalk. They each had an elaborate hairstyle. One girl had bright yellow curls cascading over her shoulders although the front of her hair was jet black. Another had long red streaks in her hair. And the third girl was downright scary. She had magenta braids—hundreds of them, coiled like snakes on her head. A real-life Medusa. They all wore the same kind of too-tight jeans and snug shirts that squeezed their breasts out the top. And they all had cell phones vibrating on their bodies as if they were battery-operated dolls.

The girls smiled at Darrio as we stopped in front of the restaurant, and Darrio said *hola* to them. I guess he ate at the restaurant often.

"Who's that?" one asked, pointing her cigarette at me.

When Darrio told them that I was his little sister just arrived from the DR, they snickered. "Oh, is that the little *princessa*?" the girl with yellow curls asked.

"Oh, the flower girl, right?" asked the girl with red highlights.

The way she said "flower girl" made me cringe.

Darrio didn't seem to notice anything in their voices, or if he did, he didn't act on it.

"You better take her shopping, Darrio. She looks like she just walked off the beach at Boca Chica," said the snake girl.

Although their words were salted in giggles, I didn't laugh. They weren't sharing any jokes with me.

Darrio looked down at me and then at them. "Yes, we do need to shop, don't we, *princessa*?"

I nodded, but deep down I was wondering how those girls could stand being wrapped up so tightly in their shiny cellophane clothes. I hoped Dario didn't expect me to wear that. Trickles of sweat ran down my back under my T-shirt.

"Don't worry, *muchacha*," said the snake girl as she snuffed out her cigarette. "We came from the island a few years ago, too. You'll learn, just like we did."

For the first time, I felt something like fear. I shuddered despite the heat, and Darrio squeezed my hand.

Our next stop was the high school. The doors were big

and bronze, and the building was massive like a fort. *Okay, Nina. This is it.* Maybe I hoped to find something different here to make up for all I had left behind. Something worth traveling all this way.

While Darrio answered questions and filled out forms, I looked around at the cluttered main office. Over a hundred mail slots lined one wall. There was a typed name on a white label below each, and I figured out these were the names of the teachers. I couldn't imagine so many teachers in an entire city in the DR, let alone in one school.

As I sat there, the bell shrieked loudly and the hallways reverberated with the sounds of students barging through the corridors, like waves rolling onto the shore.

Darrio and I waited for the assistant principal, who came out of her office to shake our hands. She spoke to me in Spanish but I answered in English, and she looked pleased. Her name was Mrs. Cordelia, and she was dressed in a suit and had a nice face. Still, there was a hard edge to her.

Darrio handed over my documents: my passport, health certificates, and other papers, which I did not recognize. They spoke about getting my transcript from my old school in Samana, and Mrs. Cordelia said she would personally take care of it.

Then Mrs. Cordelia asked me if I was on a vocational or academic track.

"I don't know."

"Well, what kinds of classes would you be interested in, Nina?"

I was confused, because I thought you just went to school and that was it. But now this lady was asking me if I wanted science and math or creative and artistic subjects or computers and health. I looked at Darrio for help, and he shrugged his shoulders.

"Well, do you have any idea what you would like to do after high school?"

"She's going to college," Darrio interjected.

"That means she will have to go to summer school to get caught up on all her subjects. Then we can put her in our new IB program next September. It is a wonderful college prep program." Mrs. Cordelia smiled at me, and I felt trapped. How could I tell her in front of Darrio that I was leaving New York as soon as possible? My plan was to go back to my life as the flower girl again, even if my garden had withered and died because Mami forgot to water my plants as she'd promised. I had to go back.

Darrio asked Mrs. Cordelia what the IB program was,

and I sat fiddling with the hem of my skirt. After Mrs. Cordelia had explained it slowly and patiently, she asked, "Do you think you would want to do that, Nina?"

I nodded and Darrio nodded, too, as if he were the one who was going to be doing all that geometry and French and astronomy and English literature.

"Do you grow any plants here?" I suddenly burst out.

Mrs. Cordelia looked surprised. A frown rippled up her forehead. "Do you mean gardening? Landscaping?"

I nodded, but now I felt foolish for asking. This was school; of course they didn't have a garden here.

"Sorry, Nina, no flowers here. But that does not mean you cannot do something for a school project with your science teacher. Why don't you discuss it with her when you start school on Monday?"

"Really? You think I can grow a garden for school?"

"Well, let's discuss it with your teacher first. But we encourage independent study with the IB program. Maybe this could be a part of it."

I looked over at Darrio and smiled my first real happy smile. Darrio looked almost relieved.

"You're all set, Nina," Mrs. Cordelia said as we stood up to leave. "See me on Monday morning and I will give you your class schedule, and we will see if you belong in tenth grade for the rest of the year. Then we can discuss summer school after that."

"Thank you, Mrs. Cordelia." I held out my hand to shake hers.

As Darrio and I walked down the hallways and back out the bronze door, my heart began beating loud and fast. The school yard held an army of kids. More than an army, more like an entire ocean of teenagers all pushing each other, swearing, and laughing so shrilly that my ears hurt. And as I looked around, there was not one tree, not one flower in sight.

I wondered if Mrs. Cordelia was just being nice when she said I could grow flowers for school.

I followed Darrio without a word. We made our way back to the big river of St. Nicholas Avenue, and then to Darrio's building—a brown giant. I looked up as we walked into the dark building. I caught a glimpse of clouds, a piece of sky, and a bird flying away just as the door slammed behind me and the black elevator box opened up for us.

8

MY DAYS BEGAN TO form a pattern, but like dominoes lined up neatly in a row, there was a profound feeling that one single mistake would cause everything to collapse in a heap. Every morning, Darrio gave me money and told me to walk safely to school and to stop at the *colmado* on the way home to buy food or anything else I needed. I had to pass in front of the barbershop every day, and I held my breath each time wondering if I would see the tall boy with the green eyes again. I couldn't stop thinking about his warm hand on my arm. When I got near the red-and-white barber poles, I slowed down, glancing casually into the windows. Mami would scream at me if she knew, but there was nothing to stop me.

Once, the door was open and I glanced inside and saw him standing at a red barber chair, his dark hair curling up at the edges of his T-shirt. His back was turned to me, but I knew it was him. I hesitated in the doorway, my pupils like pinpoint magnets forcing him to turn around and look at me. He was holding shears in one hand, and he nodded briskly at me. I waved my hand at my side and scooted away quickly. I imagined that his green eyes followed me as I walked off.

Stop being silly. Stop acting like those girls back home, walking past boys' homes, hoping to see them come outside. But I couldn't help the small shiver that rippled through me at seeing him again.

I learned that St. Nicholas Avenue in the Heights is officially named Juan Pablo Duarte Boulevard after one of the Dominican Republic's founding fathers. This was truly our street—we Dominicanos who had moved to New York, one after the other in a great tidal wave of migration northward. I felt proud and sad at the same time. It was another reminder of home, but also a sign that we were here to stay—and that meant me, too.

I didn't like walking home alone on the wide street. The

But Darrio didn't explain. Just like he didn't explain when I asked him where he worked. It was during my first week and we were having dinner at the small fold-up table.

He chewed his food slowly, swallowed, wiped his mouth on a napkin, cut up some more chicken, and finally mumbled that he worked for the landlord.

"Who?"

Darrio finished his mouthful of food. "I work for the man who owns this building."

"What do you do for the owner?"

Darrio heaved a big sigh as if I was bothering him. "When I first came to New York I didn't have any place to live. So this man offered me a job and said I could live here rent free. So I took it."

"So you are like the maintenance man for the building?"

"Yeah, sort of."

"You take care of the building, and you don't have to pay rent? That sounds like a good deal."

"I guess." He was looking at the wall and not at me. I knew there was more, but Darrio was not saying.

I had to ask one more question.

"Darrio, are you happy here?"

Silence. Darrio got up and carried his plate to the

kitchen. I heard water running in the sink and the refriger-ator door opening and closing. There was the pop of a soda can or a beer bottle. Darrio leaned against the counter, his back to me. He wasn't going to answer my question, but it didn't matter. His silence told me much more than any words could have.

Perhaps Darrio hadn't adapted to this place like I'd thought. Maybe he was still wishing, even after ten years, to be able to go home to Samana. That thought made me more homesick than ever. All I knew was that the New York I had been dropped into was not the Neuva York I had expected.

That night, I closed my eyes and imagined I was sit-ting under the calabash on our hill. With the lovely ocean breezes caressing my skin, and the uplifting clove fra-grance of the leaves near my face, none of this was real.

9

AMERICAN HIGH SCHOOL WAS just like the television shows starring beautiful girls and boys with swagger, overly bright colors, and noises that popped and fizzled. The hallways streamed fashions, iPods, sneakers, laptops, and pretty teenagers acting like animals. It was made for TV. After the emptiness of Darrio's apartment, it was a pot boiling over with excitement.

On my first day, I got my schedule from Mrs. Cordelia. I tried to hide in the back of my classes, but the teachers introduced me to the students and made me sit up front. Some teachers even gave me tests and quizzes to see what I knew, and I scribbled fast and breathed even faster trying to get through that first day. As the new girl I couldn't hide for long, and by the end of the first day at least ten kids had asked me if I had just arrived from the DR. One girl came right out and asked me if I had a man yet.

"Umm, no," I shook my head. I actually smiled at her expression. She looked surprised.

"You are so pretty," she declared in a bubbly voice. "You could be a model! But how come you don't wear any makeup?" Before I could respond, she continued. "I can do a makeover for you if you want." She pulled out makeup brushes and waved them around like they were magic wands.

I started to shake my head, but then I stopped. This was a chance to make a friend. I shouldn't be so quick to say no. So, instead, I smiled at her and told her my name.

"I'm Bunny," she said.

"Bunny? Is that your real name?"

"Yeah! My mom read it in a book."

"I hope it wasn't *Runaway Bunny*."

Bunny didn't laugh. "It was."

"Oh my God. I'm so sorry. I didn't mean to make fun of your name." What a way to start a new friendship.

"That's okay, it's not so bad being named after a

famous children's book, I guess."

"No, it isn't. It shows your mom was reading while she waited for you. I love that story anyway. At least she didn't give you the Spanish name for bunny and call you *conejito*."

Bunny and I walked down the hallway laughing, and it felt so good to be able to laugh over something silly.

That first week Bunny and I ate lunch together in the school yard because it was too hot to eat inside the cafeteria. Bunny was turning out to be a real matchmaker, as she was constantly pointing out a potential "perfect man" for me. I told her over and over that I was not interested, but she kept trying anyhow. I was forced to look at her choices and shake my head at each and every one of them. I didn't know if Mr. Green Eyes went to my school, but I kept an eye out for him.

Bunny and I were complete opposites. I was shy and read at lunch, but Bunny was a social butterfly with no real landing place. She flitted here and there, laughing and talking with everyone. But she always came back to fill me in on who was who and what was happening. What I liked most about Bunny was that she knew what she wanted to be. Bunny only attended our school in the mornings. After lunch, she took a bus to another school where she took dance classes in the afternoons. I loved listening to her talk about dancing because her eyes lit up and her voice got high-pitched. She reminded me of myself when I was planning something new for my garden and used to tell Darrio all about it on the telephone from Samana. I hung out with Bunny every day at school, and kept to myself after she left in the afternoons.

Then, during my second week at school, a boy I'd never noticed before sat right next to me and offered me a chocolate Pop-Tart from his shirt pocket. I stared at the shiny foil wrapper in silence.

"It's okay, everyone eats in class," he whispered.

"No thanks." I was too shocked to say anything else. The boy acted as if we'd known each other forever.

He shrugged his shoulders and took a big bite of a Pop-Tart, wiping crumbs from the side of his face. "You're missing out."

I wished Bunny was there. She'd probably take the Pop-Tart and joke with the boy. For the first time I wished I was more like Bunny, laughing and joking about everything, instead of being so serious all the time.

I went back to reading *The Glass Menagerie* by Tennessee

Williams. Our teacher had said that we would be acting out parts in the play by the end of the semester, and I needed to understand many of these new English words.

The boy wouldn't give up. After class, he leaned over and asked for my cell phone number. I told him I didn't have a cell phone. "No phone?" He shook his head. "Who are you?"

That was the exact question I asked myself every morning in this new world, but I didn't say that to him. "You don't need my number because you know exactly where to find me every day at this time." Then I got up, gathered my backpack, and hurried away before I blushed too much.

Every day the boy sat next to me in English and offered me Pop-Tarts and peanut butter crackers, until one day I couldn't refuse. I finally broke down and began chatting with him.

His name was Carlos, and we talked about *The Glass Menagerie*, which strangely reminded me of my own family. The mother in the play, Amanda, sounded like Mami, wanting a rich man for her daughter, Laura, to marry. Tom, her son, was stuck taking care of his mother and sister, although he longed to travel. And then there was

Laura herself, playing with little glass animals and afraid to live in the real world.

"What do you think of Laura?" I asked Carlos before class.

He munched on a Pop-Tart. "She's the most tragic of them all."

I shivered. "Why? It's not her fault she has to wear a brace on her leg, and it makes her shy."

"No, that's not why. She's tragic because she lives only in this fantasy world—with her glass animals. She has no real life."

"Well, her mother is certainly trying to get her a life. But marrying her off to a rich man won't get her a *real* life."

"Ha! Tell that to these girls at school. They all want a guy with a nice ride who wears fancy jewelry and who can buy them things."

I bit my lips. Then I noticed Carlos staring, so I stopped. Bunny had said that Carlos liked me, but I ignored her. I wasn't sure whether Mami would call this flirting because all Carlos did was feed me Pop-Tarts and talk about books and school and things that made me feel I was learning much more from him than from the teachers. He was definitely the smartest boy in our class. He was taking AP classes in physics and chemistry, and when I asked him if he was already thinking of college, he said no, he was already thinking of medical school. I had never met anyone who was planning to go to medical school. He was from our capital, Santo Domingo. Maybe the big-city kids thought of medical school because there was one right there.

Carlos turned to face the teacher as class started. "You are just like the glass unicorn in the menagerie."

"Me? But it breaks."

"What does that tell you?" And he gave me a strange smile.

How was I like the unicorn? I wasn't fragile. I didn't live in a make-believe world. I shook my head and a long curl fell into my eyes.

Then a thought made me slump back in my chair. If Tennessee Williams had portrayed characters exactly like Mami and Darrio in his play, had he also portrayed me, too? Was I Laura, whom Carlos called the most tragic one of all?

I flipped open my book and stared at the words traveling up and down the pages, revealing secrets of a family I didn't know at all.

IO

THE DAYS WERE GETTING even hotter and many of
the stores along St. Nicholas Avenue began to leave their
doors open. Now when I walked by Angel's Barbershop,
I could see Mr. Green Eyes cutting hair, shaving faces,
shaking his barber smock out, and always he would sense
me there and turn around. He never said anything, he just
nodded his head and I would wave back. I don't know if he
was shy like me, but something had to happen. I was filled
with bubbles of anxiety that were ready to erupt.

One day I was shocked to see Green Eyes outside leaning against the pole, his arms crossed on his chest as if he
was lounging there waiting for someone. I stopped in my

tracks. Even from half a block away I could feel his eyes pulling me forward like invisible strings.

There was nothing warm and friendly about him, but I looked up at his carved, icy face and said the first thing that came to my mind: "Will you cut my hair?" And just like that, he revealed a dimple in one cheek and a light in his eyes.

He reached out and touched my hair, picking up a curl and weighing it in his hand. Then he laid it back down gently on my shoulder. "No, I'm not going to cut your hair."

"Why not?"

"Because you'll regret it."

I didn't know what to say next. All I knew was that I didn't want to leave.

"You want a soda?" he asked, straightening up and heading inside the shop.

He went to a corner and opened a small fridge. "Come on," he called as I hovered by the door not daring to step inside. "Coke or Sprite?"

He was holding out two sodas.

"Coke, please."

He wiped the top of the can, then popped it open and handed it to me with a straw.

"Sit down." He pointed to his plushy red chair.

"You don't have any customers?"

He took a big gulp of soda. "This is my new break time."

I sank back against the high chair, feeling as if I was in a fairy tale. Mirrors ran the length of the room from the middle of the wall to the ceiling. Built-in shelves held scissors, combs, brushes, and shaving equipment. Bottles of oils and lotions were neatly lined up on one shelf. It was his world, and I looked at myself in the mirror, seeing a girl I barely recognized. My lips were moist and red and my cheeks flushed from the heat of his closeness. "I'm Nina," I blurted.

"I know. I'm Luis Santana. Your brother doesn't like me, Nina."

I was taken aback by his words.

"Why doesn't he like you?"

"Why are you here? You don't really want a haircut."

I looked down at my hands turning the soda can around and around. "To meet you, I guess." For sure, Mami would yank me out of this chair, and I'd never be able to leave the house. But I wasn't doing anything except talking.

Luis Santana revealed that incredible dimple again. "I wanted to meet you, too."

"Are all those haircuts done by you?" I pointed to a pinup board featuring photos of fancy fades with geometric patterns that looked incredibly complicated.

He nodded. "I design them myself. It's my specialty here."

He wasn't boasting, but I could hear the pride in his voice. "Now that one I'd like," I said, pointing to a bird on the side of a boy's head. Luis grinned. Then, like the wind changing course, he sobered up. "We can't be friends, Nina. You know that."

"Why not?" I shifted in the chair. Was he going to tell me he had a girlfriend? He probably did, with his handsome face and glittery eyes.

"Just take my word for it."

"And what if I want to be friends?" I surprised myself.

He stopped fiddling with his soda can and stared at me. "Believe me, it's not a good idea. Ask your brother."

My stomach churned from the cold Coke and his chilled words.

The other barbers were ignoring us, chatting loudly with each other, changing the channels on the TV for the customers, and counting out change.

One thing I had learned about growing a garden is

patience. You had to wait and see what would develop.

The next day, Luis was standing outside the barbershop when I walked by on my way home. Without discussing what we were doing, he offered me a soda and helped me with my heavy backpack. Then I climbed into the barber chair and we chatted for fifteen minutes until his break was over. We didn't talk about the past or the future. I told him about school, and he told me about his customers. For two wonderful weeks, Luis waited for me to walk by. If it was raining, he waited by the door, but always he was there and I felt the blossoming of something remarkable, something that made me almost glad I was here in Neuva York.

II

ONE DAY I ASKED Darrio why he didn't give me enough money to buy food for several days. It would be easier than having to walk into the *colmado* every day, trying not to look at the drug dealers.

Darrio snapped at me. "It's complicated." I didn't know what he meant, but I didn't argue about it, either.

I soon realized that I would learn more by staying quiet than by asking a lot of questions. That was how I noticed the constant ringing of the doorbell throughout the evenings and on weekends, too. At first I didn't know what the noise was. But after watching for a while, I began to see a pattern. Darrio would press a button by the wall, walk out the door, and disappear down the hall. I assumed he was going to let in a friend or girlfriend, but he never came back with anyone. When I asked who it was, he always said the same thing, "Not important, *mi amor*."

One day after the buzzer had rung three times in an hour, I had to ask him again.

"What's going on, Darrio?" I kept my voice soft. And I wondered why I was being *timida* with my own brother.

He shook his head. "I told you it's nothing, *princessa*." He pressed his lips together tightly. His eyelids slid down like shutters closing in my face.

Something felt *muy malo* here.

One day after Darrio hurried out, I tiptoed over to the door and opened it slowly. Darrio was putting a key into a door down the hall. A man was standing next to him. Darrio pushed open the door, and they walked into the room together. I closed our door quietly and leaned against it. Something very strange was going on. Who was that man? Was he the one who rang five times a day? Why did Darrio have a key for that room? And why didn't Darrio want me to know? The more I thought about it, the more puzzled I grew. My head felt as if it was bursting with questions. His secret was like a balloon growing bigger around me, threatening to pop. Part of me was afraid to examine it too closely because of what I might find out.

12

IT WAS SEÑORA RIVERA from the *colmado* who gave me the idea to start growing flowers right here in the Heights.

She told me about her hometown of Jarabocoa in the República Dominicana with its many waterfalls and tall, green mountains. Señora Rivera told me about the dwarfs who lived at the base of the mountains and grew lovely scented orchids. "That's what I miss the most, Nina."

"What?" I asked, sitting on the stool she offered me next to the register.

"The orchids!" She closed her eyes as if she were seeing them in her mind. "The mountains were filled with all different kind of orchids, and their scents could wake up a sleeping giant. My favorite was called 'lady of the night' and you could smell them through your bedroom window."

I was falling under the spell of her memory as I imagined the orchids blooming with their delicate petals. Then I told her about my garden of tropical flowers and roses in Samana. "But I never grew orchids before."

Señora Rivera put her hand over her heart. "Oh, *mi corazón*, I love *flores*."

"Me too," I said. "Me too."

I decided right then and there to try and grow flowers in Darrio's apartment. I would have to talk to my brother. He would know how to do it. And I would bring some for Señora Rivera. I was so excited about having something real to do in this place where nothing seemed real to me that I went home to get started right away.

"Darrio!" I barged through the door, and swung my backpack off my shoulders. Darrio was not there, so I went to my room and started drawing ideas for an inside garden. I walked around our apartment and peeped into Darrio's bedroom and saw that there was absolutely no light in that room. The kitchen had no windows, and the living room windows faced another building, so there was not much light there, either. I went back to my bedroom and sat on my bed and tapped my pencil on my notebook. It was hot, so I went to open the window and as I pushed up the heavy-paned glass, I saw the black metal landing outside and I gasped. That was it. I leaned out the window carefully and glanced all around. It really was the only place where flowers could get some light. But whoever heard of flowers in the sky?

I stood looking out the window for about ten whole minutes. Then I took a deep breath and gingerly put one foot out the window. My heart was hammering so much I thought I would lose my balance and fall. I reached out my hands and grasped the metal landing and pulled myself out all the way until I was kneeling on the landing. The ground was far below.

Bit by bit, I raised my body up until I was standing on the landing. I squared my shoulders and let out a big breath. And suddenly, in a burst of welcome, the clouds drifted apart and the sun's rays fell on my shoulders. It was not strong like it was back home, but it was still the same sun. Darrio had been right. This was the best part of our home.

I was still on the fire escape when I heard our front door open and close, and I knew that Darrio had come back home. "Darrio. Come see this."

"Nina, where are you?'

"Out here on the fire escape."

Darrio came into my bedroom and hurried over to my window. "So you decided to try it out, *princessa*?"

I nodded excitedly. "Darrio, I want to start growing something."

Darrio frowned. I didn't want him to say no, so I kept talking. "Maybe orchids, what do you think?"

Darrio climbed out on the fire escape with me and looked around. He put one hand under his chin like he was considering the idea.

"Why not? We can grow orchids right here in flowerpots."

"Really?"

"Yes, they don't need direct sunlight, so this is perfect, and there's enough air movement for them to grow. Plus, orchids don't even require dirt. We can use bark."

"Bark?"

"Tropical orchids grow in the air instead of in soil."

"Flowers that grow in the air? You're kidding me."

But Darrio wasn't joking. "Yup, they attach themselves to peat moss or fir bark or even coconut fiber. They don't need to be rooted in the earth."

"We're really going to have a garden in the sky. That's perfect!"

"Yes, little sister." I high-fived him, charmed that he sounded like my big brother again.

I pushed aside any dark thoughts of Darrio and focused instead on our plan. "When can we start?"

"I'll get everything we need while you're at school. How's Friday?"

I nodded my head vigorously.

"Okay, come on. We're going out to celebrate."

I took one last look around the fire escape. Maybe this garden would change Darrio back to the way he was in Samana, digging holes and trimming leaves. And if Darrio was his old self, I could stop feeling so nervous around him. Maybe I could ask the questions that tugged at my mind all day long.

I jumped back inside my bedroom as if I had been going in and out of the window all my life. I felt as if I could jump right down to the street. "Where are we going, Darrio?" I asked. I looked down at my cotton sundress and sandals, then back at him. I had one of Bunny's sweaters tied around my waist for the chilly mornings, so I untied it and began brushing my hair. Darrio still had not taken me shopping.

"Well, the Latin Star, of course. I promised you *sancocho*, and tonight that is the special."

My stomach grumbled at the idea of the delicious stew, but my heart dropped at the idea of going to the Latin Star. Those girls were always hanging out front and they teased me relentlessly, calling me "*princessa*" and "little flower girl." They made fun of my island clothes. I hated to walk past them, and now Darrio wanted to take me right into their little hornet's nest.

"Umm, ummm . . . Darrio. I was hoping to cook dinner tonight. Can we stay home instead?"

"Is there something wrong, Nina?" he asked suspiciously.

"Nope," I lied right to his face. "I just want us to stay home and eat dinner here."

He shook his head and screwed up the side of his mouth as if he knew I was not telling him the truth.

I felt a twinge of guilt for spoiling our happy mood. But I couldn't let Darrio know that the girls tormented me.

So both of us were hiding things from each other now. But in truth, it was Darrio who had the real secret.

13

ON FRIDAY AFTERNOON, DARRIO brought home five orchids in plastic pots. None of them had any blooms, and I was anxious to see what the flowers would look like.

"Are we going to repot them?" I asked, looking inside the bags he had put down in my bedroom. I didn't see any new pots.

Darrio shook his head. "Wait here, let me change my clothes."

I looked at the dry, leathery plants and wondered how anything beautiful would come out of them. Darrio came back wearing an old T-shirt I remembered, with rips and holes and stains that Mami could never get out. I laughed at him. "Darrio, what is that?"

He looked down. His dark eyes crinkled up in the corners and a light shone in them. He braced his legs apart and opened the window to the fire escape.

"Come help, *princessa*," he said as he climbed out the window.

I handed him the pots of orchids one by one, and Darrio placed them on the fire escape. Darrio spread his arms wide as if embracing the sky. For a moment, he looked like he was standing on the hillside next to our pink wooden house, free and happy, instead of standing on a cramped fire escape over New York City.

I climbed out the window, too, and began examining the plants. "How long before they bloom?"

"They've all bloomed for the year already. They bloom from December through May, so I got them at a good price."

"But I wanted to have flowers over the summer." I tried not to sound disappointed.

"Well, that's where you get to show your true talents, *princessa*. Because with the right pruning, you can make new blooms appear again."

I looked over at Darrio, who was kneeling next to me

now. "You have to prune them carefully," he instructed.

Darrio showed me the spikes where flowers had just dropped off. "Find the small fleshy bumps or nodes on the plant near the spikes. Count three nodes, then cut the spike an inch above the third node. Make sure and count the green fleshy nodes, not the dried-out ones."

I examined the spikes and counted, then I reached for the pruning tool and snipped carefully. I did two more, feeling for the nodes and checking that they were green ones.

"Wow, Nina, you got this."

I sat back on my heels. "It's what I do," I joked.

We continued counting nodes and snipping the spikes and getting our orchids in perfect shape for more blooms. I was determined to have flowering orchids for Señora Rivera soon.

"When do we repot them?" I looked at the boring plastic pots they were sitting in.

"Hopefully never! Orchids hate to be uprooted. They'll act up and won't flower for a year or more. They're happy staying right where they are."

I knew how they felt. Darrio was quiet, too, as if he could read my mind. We finished up on the fire escape and climbed back inside as the sun was just starting to slip behind a building.

After we settled the orchids on the fire escape, Darrio and I walked to La Nacional to send Mami money. We did this every Friday, and while Darrio counted out money for the clerk and filled out the proper forms, I enjoyed the cool air-conditioning and the sights of people walking by with happy faces because the weekend had begun. The barbershop was on the same block, so I kept my eye out for Luis. I'd noticed that Friday was the busiest day for the barbers, so I never expected to see Luis when I walked by with Darrio, which was a good thing since I had not mentioned Luis to him yet.

"Darrio, do you ever get a haircut at Angel's?" It had suddenly occurred to me that Darrio could walk in while I was sitting in the barber chair.

"Yes, every other week, why?"

I played with the ends of my hair. "Where will I get a haircut?" I stammered, trying to think of a good reason.

This time Darrio stopped walking and I almost bumped into him. "Do you need a haircut?" His face was dead serious as if I'd told him I needed an operation.

"Maybe. Mami always trimmed my hair herself."

"We can ask the girls at the Latin Star," he said, pointing at the girls outside the restaurant just up ahead.

"No way!" I shouted and then quickly covered my mouth with my hand.

At that moment I heard a sharp step behind me like someone was very close, and I turned around. It was Luis. My heart did a flip just like the first time I saw him.

Luis didn't say anything, just stared at me.

Darrio hadn't noticed that I had stopped walking behind him. It was just me and Luis on the sidewalk, and I saw something glittering in his right hand. He was gripping a metal razor and tiny wisps of hair fluttered all over his hand and on his black T-shirt.

"Were you just cutting someone's hair?" I asked foolishly, as it was obvious.

"Why'd you walk by without saying hello? The door was wide open, and I waved at you."

"I'm sorry, I didn't see you," In truth I had purposely not looked inside the door.

Luis' eyes got a darker green. "You haven't told Darrio about me, have you?" We stared at each other for a moment before Darrio came tearing back to my side.

"Nina, what's going on? You know this guy?"

Before I could respond, Luis said, "No, she doesn't." I felt sick to my stomach.

Luis took out a handkerchief from his pocket and handed it to me. "Here." I didn't realize I was sweating, but suddenly my face felt very hot.

I looked down at the perfect white square with a dark red border, like a warning sign around the edges. In one swift motion, Luis turned and walked away. I hadn't said thank you. I hadn't said one word to show that I knew him. What was wrong with me?

As he opened the door to the barbershop, he looked back at me with a sharpness in his eyes and I felt pure regret.

"Nina, come on," said Darrio urgently.

St. Nicholas Avenue seemed like an empty place. When Darrio sent Mami's money, we called her. I was determined to tell her about Luis, but as soon as I heard her demanding voice, I told her about Carlos instead. I knew he would impress Mami. I told her how he was *muy inteligente* and was going to college to be a doctor. Mami got so excited she screamed in my ear, and I dropped the phone. Darrio picked it up and told Mami to calm down.

I could hear Mami instructing Darrio to buy me new

clothes so that I could look attractive! *Oh, Mami*, I wanted to say, *You sound just like Amanda in* The Glass Menagerie. Darrio listened as she told him everything she needed— more money for her foot operation, a new stove, and money to pay bills. I didn't know if it was my frustration over the Luis incident or because I was mad I couldn't tell Mami whom I really liked, but I grabbed the phone from Darrio and said, "He doesn't have that much money. Leave him alone." Darrio stared at me with his mouth wide open, and there was silence on Mami's end of the line. I was shocked, too, but before Darrio could take back the phone I said, "Bye, Mami, have a good week," and I hung it up.

"What the hell was that?" Darrio exclaimed.

"I don't know." Who was this girl, hanging out in a barbershop with a guy who was supposedly not good for her, and now hanging up on her mother?

"I'm tired of how Mami complains to you all the time. It sounds worse now that I'm here."

Darrio reached for the phone, then put it down again. "I should call her back. You can tell her you're not feeling well or something."

"I feel fine. Why don't we go home?"

Darro stared at the phone, and I could practically see

him fighting with himself. I felt sorry for him. Mami was not going to change. He finally let out a sigh and we walked out the store together. "*Muchacha*, you are starting to scare me."

"Yeah, I'm starting to scare myself."

14

I SPENT THE ENTIRE weekend feeling like I was in a prison, but the bars were my own thoughts. I couldn't study or watch TV. I burned dinner and spilled an entire pitcher of lemonade. I worried about what would happen on Monday when I had to walk by the barbershop. How would I tell Luis I was sorry? I wished Monday would come quickly so I could get this over with. I also worried about Mami. On Monday, I unleashed all my torment on Bunny.

Bunny was uncharacteristically levelheaded. "*Chica,* you got to decide whose life you want to live, your own or your mother's." That was easy for Bunny to say. Her mother supported her dream of being a dancer and wasn't trying to marry her off. Bunny could go on dates and talk to guys on her phone whenever she wanted.

"I'm not saying you should totally dis your mother," Bunny continued. "Just let her know that you want to choose who you want. And no one likes secrets, so you should be straight with her and with Darrio."

I knew she was right. "But what should I do about Luis?"

Bunny closed her eyes and swayed back and forth, going into her dramatic mode again. "Star-crossed lovers, so romantic."

"You're no help."

Her eyes snapped at me. "Just tell him you're sorry. What you did was dumb. It sounds like he really likes you, and you hurt his feelings."

"I feel horrible."

"You should. Stop with the secrets."

Bunny was right. It was time for me to stand up for myself. And honestly, how could Mami expect me to be the same little flower girl up here? Everything was different.

After school, I hurried out the gates, anxious to get to the barbershop and make everything right with Luis again. But the door was closed. I peered in the windows but Luis was not by his barber chair. On Tuesday it was the same thing. On Wednesday, I was strangling myself with nervousness, so I boldly pushed open the door and went in. "Luis, *no esta*," said one of the barbers. He wasn't there. I wondered where he was.

I murmured *gracias* and left. Every day I walked by and felt the same churning excitement at seeing him, followed by an increasingly hollow feeling when I didn't. I had really messed this up, and I didn't know how to fix it.

15

THE NEXT FRIDAY, I was following Darrio to La Nacional when the girl with yellow curls yanked my scarf off my head. I slipped and cried out as my shin hit the concrete.

"No me moleste," I said in frustration at the girls.

"Awww, the little flower girl is crying," teased the one with red hair.

The girls flicked their cigarette ashes at me. "Go tell your big brother on us, little *princessa*," said Medusa.

As I turned to follow Darrio into the money store, a shiny, white Jeep pulled up next to the curb and distracted them. I slipped inside, where Darrio was already counting out his money for Mami, and looked out the big glass window.

Out of the vehicle stepped Luis. I couldn't believe it. It was really him! His black hair was slicked back, and the ends curled up around his ears. His eyes shone like green shards of light. He was wearing a black T-shirt and jeans, and he walked like he was out of a movie. As he opened the door, he looked right at me.

"Hello." His voice was seawater pooling in my head. I couldn't even answer. My tongue was cement in my mouth, and my scarf slipped through my fingers. Before it touched the floor, he bent over and caught it. He held it out to me like it was something precious.

"Thank you," I said softly, looking up. Out of the corner of my eye, I saw Darrio rest the phone on his shoulder and look at me disapprovingly.

I don't know if Luis saw Darrio's face, but he walked toward the counter and went on with his business. Before he left, he turned to look at me again, but this time he had a frown on his face.

"I'm sorry," I said. He gave me a fake smile and left the store.

I watched as the three *muchachas* smiled at him and

touched his shoulders flirtingly. He did not stop to talk. He gave them a little wave as he climbed into his white Jeep and started the engine. Before he took off, he looked once more into the store window. I placed my hand flat on it as if to say good-bye, but what I really meant was "come back." He acted like he couldn't wait to get away from me. As he drove off, I felt for the first time that feeling that Mami had told me about; the feeling that made girls do foolish things.

Just being near Luis, I felt like I was standing on the edge of a cliff, and I wasn't sure how to get down.

16

ON SATURDAY NIGHTS, DARRIO'S friends came over and played dominoes on the card table set up in the the living room. The men drank a lot of beers and slapped down dominoes hard and fast. The sound echoed through the walls to my bedroom, where I lay on the bed wishing I were at home dancing merengues between the rosebushes.

One Sunday morning while I helped Darrio clean up the remnants of his late-night party, I asked him, "When will I see the real New York?"

Darrio looked at me with a furrowed brow. "This *is* the real New York, Nina."

"This is Washington Heights, no?"

"Yes." He drummed his fingers on the card table.

"Well, when will I see the New York where there is lots of money and where there are rich baseball players that I am supposed to meet?"

Darrio's white teeth flashed in a grin. "You are joking?"

I shook my head slowly. "No."

"This is it, Nina. This is all there is."

I stood still. This couldn't be right. Darrio burst out laughing. Then he got up and wrapped his arms around me in a big hug.

"*Mi amor*, I will take you to Yankee Stadium to the baseball games if you want. But I don't know any players and neither does anyone else around here. The only rich folks we know are on their way to the devil's door."

I didn't like what Darrio was saying. "What do you mean?"

My brother shrugged. "It's complicated."

That same Sunday, Darrio knocked on my bedroom door. On his shoulder was a bag that looked very heavy, and by his feet were several plastic bags with plant bulbs sticking out. I jumped up to peek inside the bags.

"You found more orchids on a Sunday?" I asked.

"I got a friend to drive me up to a nursery in the Bronx. I thought you needed a little extra beauty around here."

Darrio handed me a pink-handled spade. I looked over and smiled at my brother as we worked together filling the orchids' pots with the bark and perlite mixture. Two of the orchids were in full bloom and their striped-pink petals dazzled me.

I pressed my face to the plants and inhaled their essence. "This is wonderful, Darrio."

"Better than baseball players?"

"Yes, they are!"

"*Princessa*, I should have done this a long time ago," Darrio said as he looked at our potted plants on the fire escape. A flash of sadness crossed his features, and I picked up one of the pink gardening gloves and threw it at him. "I don't need these!" I said, disgusted.

Darrio shrugged. "You are a young lady now, you might want to keep your nails clean."

I scoffed and threw the other glove at him. Darrio laughed. "Okay, then *I'll* wear it," he said, as he put on one pink glove and danced the Michael Jackson moon dance.

I was hysterical with laughter. "Don't knock over the orchids."

I squatted on the black fire escape, high above the street, and scooped more potting mixture into the flowerpots. As I dug my hands into the mix, the sun was slinking behind one of the tall buildings on St. Nicholas Avenue. I began to whistle an old merengue. If I slanted my eyes away from the street, I could imagine myself at home wiping my dirty hands on my shorts and waiting for Mami to call me in for dinner.

I glanced over at Darrio as he worked with me. I wondered if he was also thinking about our first garden. It was at that moment that the door buzzer sounded loudly, startling me and causing Darrio's head to snap up. His eyes were wide and fearful.

Darrio leaped to his feet and hurried back into the apartment, dropping the gloves and spade. I slowly turned and followed my brother's movements as he hurried to his bedroom. I hopped through the bedroom window and listened at my door. His footsteps hurried past me as I leaned against the door without breathing. Then our front door slammed closed. I bit my lip. Should I go look? What if he caught me spying on him?

Before I knew it I was standing at the front door. I held my breath and eased it open. Darrio was at the end of the hall next to the elevator. The elevator doors creaked open. Two men walked out and shook hands with him. Then Darrio gestured them over to the same door and pulled out a key. A thought suddenly struck me: that key must be somewhere in his closet. That's why he goes there every time the buzzer rings. My hand trembled as it gripped the doorknob.

The three men slipped inside the room, and I heard the loud *click* of the door closing. What was in that room? And why did he look so frightened when the buzzer rang today?

I had to get the key when Darrio was out of the apartment.

I waited some more, watching to see what else would happen. My heart beat fast, like it was racing out of my skin.

When I couldn't take the tension anymore, I closed the

front door softly and ran back to my bedroom. I climbed out onto the fire escape.

I heard Darrio's footsteps in our apartment. It was over for now. But it would start again. Maybe today. Maybe tomorrow. But always, the exact same pattern. I leaned my head against the railing and took a deep breath. Then I turned back to my tiny flowers and tried to grab hold of that feeling I had had earlier, but it was gone.

17

DURING THE LAST WEEK of school, our English class performed scenes from *The Glass Menagerie*. Carlos and I had chosen a scene together and practiced at lunch with Bunny as our director. Bunny, Carlos, and I were becoming a little trio, but I secretly thought that Carlos wanted me all to himself. Bunny liked to tease Carlos, telling him that he had some serious competition for my heart. She would drop little hints about my barbershop guy, but I always hushed her. Besides, I had not seen Luis since the day he was in his Jeep. He was avoiding me, or worse, had forgotten about me completely.

On the last day of school, Bunny told Carlos that he'd

better act fast. She said that I would end up picking Mr. Green Eyes and ruin my mother's dream of having a doctor in the family.

"Bunnyyyyyyy!"

"Whaaaaaaaat?"

Carlos rolled his eyes. "Little Miss Prim-and-Proper here with a drug dealer? That will be the day."

"What?" I shouted.

Bunny looked as surprised as I was.

"I know exactly who you girls are talking about. You think I haven't heard your stupid conversations?"

"So," said Bunny. "How does that make him a drug dealer?"

Carlos shook his head in disbelief. "I can't believe you guys don't know."

"Know what?" I asked.

"The guy is eighteen years old. He drives a brand-new Jeep Cherokee. He hangs out in the barbershop every day, and, as far as I know, he doesn't have a job other than cutting people's hair. Do the math, geniuses."

Bunny and I stood there like statues. "Is it true?"

Bunny shook her head. "I don't know."

A drug dealer? No way! He looked nothing like the

colmado kids. "Are you sure?" I asked Carlos.

Carlos shrugged. "Look, today is the last day of school, Nina. I won't know where to find you after this. So *now* will you give me your home phone number?"

I hesitated, but then scribbled Darrio's phone number on a piece of notebook paper.

"Thanks," he said. "I want to invite you to a party soon. I'll call you with the info."

"Uhhmm," Bunny cleared her throat.

Carlos sniggered. "It's a date. You want to come on our first date, too?"

I felt my face turning bright red.

"Right," said Carlos. "I got to run. My internship at the hospital doesn't start until next week, so we can hang out if you want, Nina."

"I have summer school starting in a couple of weeks, so I'm free until then."

Bunny had gotten a scholarship to a dance camp in a place called the Catskill Mountains where the dance students performed at the end of the summer. She had already invited us to come up for it. Carlos had said he would figure out a way for us to go.

After Carlos left, Bunny and I huddled together. "A

drug dealer, Nina? I don't believe it."

"Me either."

We were both silent. In this new world, people were not at all what they appeared to be. Not my brother, not Luis, and not even me. I wished I could go back to my simple walks on the *malecón* with Mami. But that girl was gone forever.

18

WITH SCHOOL OUT I didn't have any excuse to walk by the barbershop every day. My entire world narrowed down to Darrio's apartment and the *colmado* when Señora Rivera was there. Now that I was home all the time I noticed how often the buzzer went off. I had to find out what Darrio was hiding in the room down the hall. His secret was like water seeping into my lungs. I loved my brother, but I'd have to sneak around behind his back to find answers. I had to find a time when Darrio wouldn't be home. That was the tricky part. Darrio was always going in and out at odd times. Finally, I was ready.

Darrio had a girlfriend named Marla. She was from the

Dominican Republic, too, but had lived in New York for a long time. She worked every day and many nights as a home care attendant, so it was rare for her to have time off. When she did, Darrio went over to her apartment and left me alone for an entire day and most of the night. I waited patiently until Darrio told me he was going to see Marla again. It was Tuesday and I watched him shave and put on his fancy cologne and leave the apartment, whistling like a happy man.

"Nina, call me on the cell if you need anything," he said.

I waited until I knew for certain that he was long gone. Then, carefully, on my softest feet, I tiptoed into Darrio's bedroom and opened the closet, shining a flashlight into the jumble of clothes.

I studied the shelves, wondering where he would hide a small, important key. I started with one end of the closet and picked up every magazine and shirt, standing up on my toes to feel the highest shelves.

I stopped every few minutes to hold my breath and listen to make sure the apartment was completely silent. Suppose Darrio forgot something and came back? My heart beat even faster as I wondered what I'd say to him.

I opened DVD boxes and shook them. I flicked through pages of a book. A door slammed and I froze. My eyes flickered around the room looking for a hiding space. But thankfully the noise was coming from the hallway. I started my search again. Sweat poured down my back, but I couldn't stop. Where could the key be?

Then I felt it: two keys on a metal ring resting amongst his CDs and DVDs on a high shelf. One looked like the key to our own front door. The other one had a long, strange shape and numbers carved into the side of it. I put them in my pocket and quickly straightened Darrio's shelves.

I went to my room and put on black pants, a dark shirt, and tied my long hair up and covered it with a dark scarf. I looked at myself in the mirror—all I needed were some dark glasses and I would make the perfect spy.

I was shaking. Suppose there was someone actually living in there and he looked hideous, or worse, suppose there was a dead body in there. *Okay, Nina, don't be ridiculous.*

I walked down the hall fast and turned and faced the door I had seen Darrio go in. I pushed one key in, but it was the wrong one. My fingers were trembling like crazy as I jammed the other key in, looking left and right to make sure no one was coming.

Crrreeeeaaaaakkkkkkk. The sudden noise made me jump. The door opened just a bit, and cold air instantly washed over me. There was an air conditioner on in there! I shivered uncontrollably.

Down the hall, a door opened and a man walked out into the hallway toward me. I stood there terrified, wondering whether to push open the door or act like I just got off the elevator.

"Hola," mumbled the man.

He walked right past me. All was clear. I steadied my hand and pushed open the door. The door swung open easily, and I was surrounded by complete darkness. I felt along the wall for a light switch before stepping inside. I didn't feel anything, so I stepped in carefully, and then I felt the switch. I flipped it on as I pushed the door closed behind me. And there was a scene I would never forget.

Brand-new boxes of all sizes were stacked one on top of one another in towering pyramids. I couldn't see the walls, just boxes and more boxes—with pictures on them showing TVs, video game consoles, stereo systems, computers, and cell phones. Names popped out at me: SONY and Sprint and Samsung. I turned around, gazing up and up until I thought I would faint.

I don't know how long I stood there, my eyes raking over the boxes from ceiling to floor and back up again. I covered my mouth with my hand to stop any sound. The fog in my brain cleared, and images flashed through my mind of the men and Darrio coming to this room. How did all this stuff get here? And what was Darrio doing with it all?

He was in trouble. I knew now I could not ask my brother anything. I could not say one word.

19

AFTER DISCOVERING DARRIO'S SECRET, I began to
feel more and more uneasy around him. I sat on the fire
escape and tried to remember him back in Samana. After
Darrio left for New York, his flowers gave me comfort,
and I grew to love them as my own. The yellow burst
of ginger lilies reminded me of when he would pour my
orange juice at breakfast. The vibrant white lilies made
me think of how he'd puff flour in my face while we were
making a cake for Mami's birthday.

Now I had lost that connection. My idea of what was
true had been destroyed. The man who was so talented
that he could grow anything out of the roughest, hardest

soil had become someone else completely. And where was that beautiful painting of our garden we had gotten as a gift so long ago? I had asked him about it and he had said he had no idea where it was.

Something had happened to him, something had caused him to change. I wondered if Darrio had missed me and Mami and our pink home and his favorite scarlet sun-flowers, *Tithonia*, with their heart-shaped petals. Darrio told me the story of Aurora, the dawn goddess, and her boyfriend, Tithonia, and the Mexican sunflowers named after him. Those were the sunflowers I had been trying to grow before I left Samana.

As I lay my chin on the rail of the fire escape, I had a sinking feeling. What I was going through was noth-ing compared to what Darrio must have felt. He had been all alone in New York. He had had no family here, no chance to grow anything, just a never-ending obligation to take care of his mother and sister back home. What does the soul do when it's set adrift from everything it loves? Maybe Darrio was like the orchids that stopped flowering if moved.

I asked Señora Rivera the next time I saw her. "How do you find a way to be happy in New York if you miss everything back home?"

"The heart always finds its way if you let it. But you have to be *here*," she stressed. "Not far away on the island," she said, and pointed to her head.

"Okay, I'll try to love it here," I said.

"No," said Señora Rivera, "don't *try* to love it. Just look to see what there is to do right in front of you, instead of missing what you cannot do back home."

I promised her I would do just that. I would go out with my friends. I would take care of my orchids on the fire escape. I would figure out a way to help Darrio. And I'd find a way to be close to Luis again.

20

IT WAS FRIDAY EVENING, and the summer heat shimmered on everyone's faces. Most of our neighborhood was outdoors, fanning themselves. Children played in open fire hydrants spouting cool water. I had to cook with a fan blowing right on me, and I was still dripping with perspiration, my hair pinned up on my head like a turban.

Darrio and I went to send money home to Mami. It was a special Friday for me because the small lady's slipper orchid had blossomed right on my fire escape before I expected it. I planned to give it to Señora Rivera, and I couldn't wait to surprise her.

"What's that you got there?" asked one of the Latin

Star girls. Her crew peered down at my hands.

I walked quickly, trying to make it inside the store.

I pushed past them and tried to open the door, but it was too late.

I felt a hand pull on my shirt and another one tug on my hair. The flowerpot tumbled out of my hands and hit the concrete steps, shattering into a hundred small pieces. The plastic pot inside it with the flower tumbled out and rolled on its side dislodging the plant completely. My purple orchid lay like a sparkling jewel amidst the shards of pottery and bark.

There were muffled giggles as the girls covered their mouths with their hands.

"We're so sorry, *princessa*."

"It was an accident."

"It's just a flower."

I closed my eyes and clenched my fists. I had had it. As the girls laughed, my anger swirled around me like a dust cloud. I picked up a broken piece of pottery and hurled it at them. *Bam!* The snake girl jumped back as it landed at her feet. "Are you crazy?" she shouted. I would have thrown another piece, but then I smelled something heartbreaking: barbershop powder and aftershave.

I looked up and there was Luis, standing next to me, his large, brown hands carefully shaking loose pieces of bark from around my flower.

"What kind of flower is this?" he asked softly, ignoring the girls around us.

His eyes were greener than the hills back home.

"It's an orchid."

"Where'd you buy it?"

"I didn't. I grew it." My heart was beating fast. He was holding the flower in his hand so carefully.

"They can't make this, so they want to destroy it," he said, loud enough for them to hear. "Forgive them, they have inferiority complexes."

I didn't understand his words, but I felt his meaning. I nodded my head.

"It was a present for Señora Rivera at the *colmado*."

"You never told me you grew orchids."

"You never gave me the chance."

"Just like you didn't have a chance to tell Darrio about me, right?"

"I said I was sorry."

"So you've told him now?"

I was too ashamed to answer.

"I take that as a no."

"Well, I didn't know if I'd see you again."

Luis's lips pressed into a firm line. "I knew this was going to happen." He reached out his hand to me. I was mad at his comment so I brushed his hand away.

"I didn't take you for the game-playing type, Nina."

"I'll tell him right now. He's inside," I said, pointing to the money store.

Luis shook his head. "Don't bother." His voice sounded hard, but I heard something else in his tone, something sad.

I didn't get a chance to respond because Darrio came rushing out of the money store, asking lots of questions. He stared at Luis harshly.

Luis calmly told him what had happened.

"Why would they do that?" Darrio asked as he glanced at the girls leaning against the wall, smoking and humming merengue songs, pretending they knew nothing.

"*Tranquillo, tranquillo*, that's what happened, man," said Luis firmly.

Darrio frowned. "You hang out at the barbershop, right?"

"I *work* there."

"Work?" Darrio raised an eyebrow.

Luis cocked his head. "Yes, work."

"Okay," said Darrio. "It's cool. I know who you are. This is my little sister here. I got to be careful, you know."

"I know," said Luis, his green eyes flickering over to me.

Darrio cleared his throat. "Come on, Nina, let's go."

Luis nodded at me to say good-bye. Darrio was watching like a hawk, and he mumbled something out the side of his mouth.

"What did you say?" I asked.

Darrio gave me a stern look. "I said forget about him. He's not what Mami has in mind for you, *princessa*."

"Why?"

But Darrio wouldn't say. Another question he refused to answer.

21

IT WAS THE BEGINNING of July and summer school was starting soon. I was already counting down the days. Carlos called me often, and we spoke about his internship at the hospital and his plans to get out of Washington Heights.

"I'll be a doctor by the time I am twenty-five years old," he told me excitedly. "Well, a tired resident, at least," he laughed. His enthusiasm made me wonder what I might want to study. The only thing I knew was that I loved to garden. And I loved paintings. Carlos said the answer would come to me.

The first time Carlos called, Darrio asked me a lot of questions about him. I was cooking dinner, and Darrio sat at the card table watching me. I threw him a tea towel. "Come wash the dishes, Darrio. I am not your maid."

Darrio got up and crowded my kitchen space while he washed and dried dishes. "You getting all American on me now, *chica*?"

"Yup," I said, turning and poking my finger at him. "And don't put away any wet dishes, make sure they are well dried."

"Bossy, too, Ms. Americana."

"Just do a good job." As we worked together, I told Darrio all about Carlos. "Now, *him* I like," he said, adding that he still wanted to meet Carlos before I could date him.

"Well, he has not asked me out as yet, *officially*."

"Oh, he will, *mi amor*, he will!"

"How do you know that?"

"A boy calls you every day, trust me, he will ask you out. And the sooner the better, because I don't want you talking to that delinquent at the corner."

"That what?"

Darrio hesitated. "You know who I mean."

"What did you call him?" I turned off the water and stared at my brother.

"He's always on the street, *princessa*. You don't want to be with a man like that, okay?"

It was now or never. I had to tell Darrio or else I'd never have the courage, and I'd end up like Laura in the play, unable to deal with reality. Luis was honest and real and deserved better than me hiding him and our friendship.

I turned down the stove and covered my pot of boiling rice. "Darrio, you don't know Luis. I've been talking to him at the babershop and . . ." I didn't get to say any more because Darrio exploded.

"You what? Are you crazy? I was wondering why Mami thought you were on the verge of getting yourself in trouble back home. But now I see. I didn't think you'd do the same thing in New York."

"The same what?" My blood was boiling.

"You think these men only want to *talk* to you, Nina?"

"That's what Luis and I do. We talk, we laugh, and we tell each other about our day. It's not a big deal. Mami was wrong, you know. I wasn't anything close to being a *puta*!" I spat the word out. The anger I'd been keeping tamped down since the day Mami dragged me out of that chair rose up and flowed out of me like lava. "How could you even think that about me? And Mami, too? She's determined to marry me to a *rich* man. Isn't that treating me like a *puta*?"

The blood drained from Darrio's face, and he dropped the towel and walked out of the kitchen. "You're being ridiculous. You don't know Luis Santana one bit."

Whatever Luis was I'd have to find out on my own. But Darrio was being a hypocrite calling Luis a delinquent. I'd long figured out that Darrio was selling stolen merchandise from his secret room. I didn't think that he of all people should be judging anyone. And I was not going to forget about Luis. Everything seemed better when I was near him.

Our argument gave me such a headache that I went out to the *colmado* to get some aspirin. Maybe talking to Señora Rivera would help. The temperature was soaring into the high nineties, and I felt wilted and half dead. I couldn't even sleep at night. I was too scared to leave the window open in case someone crept up the fire escape, and my small fan made no breeze at all. I was even getting heat rashes on my shoulders.

Señora Rivera gave me aspirin for my headache and some cream when she saw my rashes. She gently put some on me herself. It felt so comforting to sit on the little stool near her and let her rub my shoulders.

"Señora Rivera," I asked, "does this weather last long?"

"No, Nina. Soon it will be winter and, trust me, you will not like the snow and ice and freezing rain. It's as bad as this heat. Maybe worse!"

"Then why does everyone want to be up here if the weather is so bad?"

Señora Rivera sighed. "I wish I knew, honey. But people get into habits. They get an apartment, a job, and a certain lifestyle, and they just stick with it. Once you go down a certain road, it's tough to turn back. That's why you have to be careful which road you pick." She looked pointedly at me. "And most folks are just plain scared to change their lives."

"Scared of what?"

"Of not knowing what will happen."

"Oh," I said. "Mami told me to look at New York as a chance to change my life for the better."

"Your mami sounds like a smart woman."

"But I was happy in Samana."

Señora Rivera reached out and stroked my hair with her hand. "And you could always go back there someday. But why not see what you can learn in this new place? You don't want to stay the same all your life."

22

TINY BITS OF MAGIC began to show up in my world. I caught glimpses of Luis's white Jeep in the neighborhood as I walked back and forth to summer school in the mornings and the *colmado* every day. It was like seeing a rare bird because I wasn't sure if it was real or not.

Then Señora Rivera thanked me deeply for the purple orchid that I had repotted. She was so pleased that she wrapped me in her arms and held me closely, and when she stepped back she wiped her eyes and I was shocked to see tears there. I had always thought of Señora Rivera as tough like Mami.

I began waiting for Señora Rivera to take her afternoon

break so we could sit outside and chat while we drank lemonades. It was during these breaks that I learned a lot about the neighborhood. Señora Rivera told me about her daughter, Maria, whose husband traveled back and forth to the DR because he was a phone card distributor, and her two grandchildren.

She also told me about her own husband, who had died. Now she was helping her daughter to take care of the children.

"Maria, she acts like I'm getting in the way. She says that I think I know everything."

"But you know a lot, Señora Rivera."

Señora Rivera laughed. "Isn't it funny how daughters never think their own mothers know anything?"

I blushed.

"Now, you would be a perfect daughter for me," she said.

"Why?"

But she just kept on talking, telling me how years ago there were gang wars in Washington Heights, and everyone knew someone who was in prison or who was shot and killed.

"It was all related to drugs, *mi amor*," she said, shaking

her head. "It still is. And many innocent people died."

"Wow," I said, trying to imagine.

"You could hear the sound of gunshots at all times of the day and night. Some people were shot in their own living rooms while watching television. One girl was shot and killed on her way to school."

"No!" I said in horror.

"The girl's brother went crazy. Ended up doing some bad stuff and going to jail. The mother had lost both her children. She lived in my building and I tried to take her to church with me, but she had given up on life."

"What happened to her?"

"She died. Cancer of the throat. But I think it was because she prayed to leave the earth, and God answered her prayers."

"That's terrible. What happened to the brother?"

"Oh, he's around. He's not going anywhere. Both his mother and sister are buried near here."

I was silent, thinking of what it must be like to lose everyone you loved.

"The things I see and hear right in this store every single day. Nina, you have to be careful. Everything is not how it appears."

The way I talked to Señora Rivera was how I wished I could talk to Mami. But Mami would always change the subject to discuss money or finding a husband for me.

As I was leaving the store, Señora Rivera patted my hand and leaned down to whisper in my ear, "God is watching out for you, *mi amor*, never forget that."

23

AND THEN IT HAPPENED. I had felt it building—a glance here, a whistle there, a snicker here, a few words there. I was going past the *colmado* kids too often for them to continue ignoring me.

It was Señora Rivera's day off, so I did not stay at the store long. I got the groceries I needed, and I was walking back, swinging the handles of my canvas bag that held the *plátanos* and chicken that I would cook later. I heard a low whistle coming from the boys. I glanced to my side but kept my eyes lowered. I was sure they were not whistling at me! Not while I was wearing my plain green shorts and my hair was tied up in a scarf.

My thoughts began to drift to Luis once again. The sun dazzled the sidewalk, making it look as if there were a million diamonds on the ground at my feet. That's when I noticed the pair of black leather sneakers right in front of me. They were blocking my path and I glanced up. As my eyes traveled swiftly up the baggy blue jeans and the long T-shirt, I inhaled sharply. I tried to step to the side. He looked about my age or maybe a little older.

"Hey, Mami." He smiled down at me, licking his full lips.

"Uhm, I think you're confused," I started to say. As he took one step closer, I took a step back until my back was almost up against the wall of an apartment building. He was smirking down at me, and my eyes were locked on his.

Q-que pasa?" My voice sounded as if it was coming from the bottom of the sea.

"I've been watching you, *chiquita*. Walking up and down here every day, not noticing anyone at all, going along as if you're in another world."

I gulped. My back hit the wall, and his two hands were on either side of me, palms flat against it. His breath tickled the stray hairs escaping from under my scarf. I was sweating now, and I glanced nervously to see if anyone was around so I could call for help. But the only people there were other teenage boys watching us with grins on their faces.

"Marcos, you got yourself a *novia?*"

I pulled the bag of groceries in front of me.

He chuckled. "Cute, very cute."

I decided I might as well make a run for it. I would push the groceries at him hard, then break free and run. I didn't know what I was hoping for—that maybe a *plátano* would stab him?

I closed my eyes and took a deep breath and that's when I smelled it—cool powder and aftershave lotion.

I opened my eyes and pushed the boy. He hardly moved, but his hand slid down to my shoulder and I twisted away. My scarf got caught in his fingers and, all of a sudden, the boy was not there anymore. I spun around fast, and instead of his cocky grin, the boy had a look of pain on his face. Luis Santana clenched his upper right arm in a vise grip.

"Luis!" I gasped.

Luis shook the boy and then tossed him away like he was a candy wrapper. I felt the other teenagers hovering nearby.

"We should leave," I whispered, my eyes indicating the group watching nearby.

Luis began walking straight toward them, and they backed up as he got closer. He pushed my assailant toward the group. Then he just stood there, staring them down. I could not see the expression in his eyes, but the feeling on that sidewalk made me shiver.

Luis never uttered a word. He turned around and walked back toward me. I could hear faint rumblings from the *colmado* kids, as Luis picked up my bag and took my hand.

"It's cool, man."

"We didn't know."

"It won't happen again."

"We got your back."

Luis raised his arm and waved it at them without looking back. I didn't say anything as Luis crossed the street with me. He walked alongside me, silently, until we got to my building.

Finally, when we were in front of the door, I looked up at him. I wanted to say thank you or something, but my mind was in a whirl. . . . Just his smell was intoxicating, reminding me of how happy I used to be visiting him at the barbershop every day. Luis crossed his arms in front of his chest.

"Are you always going to need rescuing?" he asked matter-of-factly.

I shook my head. "That never happened before."

"What were you thinking, Nina?" he asked.

"Hmm . . . when?" I bit my lip.

"When you were throwing your groceries at that guy?"

"Oh, I was going to push him and run."

"I see," said Luis with a little smile on his face. "That *could* have worked. But tell me, why do you hang out at that *colmado* so much?"

"How do you know that? Is it you that I see in the white Jeep parked near the corner sometimes?"

"Maybe." He smiled fully now. "Someone's got to watch out for you."

"Me? I'm not in trouble."

Luis touched one of my curls. "I've been wanting to do that again," he admitted, resting the curl back on my shoulder gently.

How in the world could this handsome young man want to flirt with me when I was dressed like this? No makeup, no lipstick, no heels, nothing. The black strands of my hair were twisted and curled in a jungle of wildness.

Luis's green eyes glittered down at me. "Those boys won't bother you anymore."

As if there was some kind of brain lapse between my thoughts and my tongue, I blurted out, "Why doesn't Darrio like you?"

Luis stepped back from me. "You said it yourself when we met," I reminded him. "But I don't know why."

"Maybe I'll tell you one day." Then he abruptly walked away. I stood on the sidewalk watching him disappear down the block, taking his time as if he owned the streets.

Okay, Nina. Don't overreact and let your imagination run away. He was only doing what anyone else would do in that situation. It's not as if he wants to date you. I mean, look at him. He's gorgeous, older, and what's up with those eyes? I bet a lot of girls have been mesmerized by them.

I went into the apartment and began seasoning the chicken and cutting up the *plátanos*. In August, I would be sixteen. I knew a lot of girls in Samana who were married at sixteen. And I knew many, married or not, who had already had babies. I wondered if I would like to be married one day. I put the chicken in the oven and went to my bedroom. I replayed the entire scene over and over in my head, starting with Luis arriving to rescue me from the *colmado* kid. He must be watching me. He always appeared whenever I needed him. He'd suddenly shown up when the Latin Star girls were bullying me, and now this. No matter what he said about us not hanging out anymore, Luis Santana seemed to be staying close by. And that was fine by me.

24

I FINALLY HAD A date. But it was not the one I wanted. Carlos had called our apartment and asked Darrio if he could take me to a family barbecue in Queens. I think I was more excited at the idea of seeing somewhere other than the Heights than of going with Carlos.

Darrio wanted to take me shopping for the party, but there wasn't enough time. So I wore my white jeans and a pretty flowered blouse and braided my hair in a high braid that swung down my back like a tail.

"Wow, *princessa*, you will blind them all with your beauty," said Darrio.

I blushed. "Stop it."

Carlos came to pick me up, and he and Darrio chatted about the hosts of the party, Carlos's cousins in Queens who were dentists.

"They are both dentists?" asked Darrio curiously.

"Yes, both of them," said Carlos, referring to his cousin Maggie and her husband. "They have their own dentist office in Queens and their own home, too," he added proudly.

"That's fantastic," said Darrio, giving me a thumbs-up signal. "Are most of their patients Dominicans?"

"I think half of them, but the other half are from the other Caribbean islands."

I could tell Darrio was impressed with Carlos, and I felt disloyal to Luis. I wished that I could like Carlos in the same way. It would make Mami happy. And if I liked Carlos, I wouldn't have to worry about the rumors of Luis dealing drugs. No matter how often I daydreamed of Luis Santana, I was always yanked back to reality by the disturbing idea that he could be involved in a world of crime. Still I knew that even though Carlos made sense for me, I was crazy for Luis. It was his face and Jeep that I looked for on the street, his powder scent that I longed to inhale.

All thoughts of Luis and Darrio left my mind as soon as Carlos and I got on the subway to Queens. Everywhere I turned, I saw cars, buses, taxis, subways, airplanes, and superfast LIRR trains heading out to Long Island.

To get there, Carlos and I rode two subways from Washington Heights then jumped into a gypsy taxi. Looking out the window, I saw flowering bushes and perfect green squares of lawns in front of the houses. There were tall, green trees and even houses with roses climbing up white lattices.

"Oh, Carlos, look at that garden," I said more than once.

I was thrilled to be out of Washington Heights with its steamy sidewalks and tough-talking kids.

Maggie's house was at the end of the block with a side and backyard, and there was a big birthday party going on.

Maggie hugged me right away and treated me like family. She was tall and slim with long, brown hair that touched her waist and a confident smile. She wrapped me right up in her skinny arms and squeezed me tightly.

"Welcome, Nina, welcome to America!" She kissed me on my cheeks and stepped back to look me up and down.

"Carlos did not tell us how beautiful you are! *Muy linda!* And thank you for coming!"

"*Gracias*, Maggie, *te gusta es mio*," I said, hugging her back. Maggie had made me feel more at home in America in five minutes than I had felt since I'd arrived. I followed her inside the house and held tightly to her hand.

Maggie's house was roomy with tall ceilings and heavy mahogany furniture pushed aside to make space for dancing. This was what I wanted to have one day: a lovely home that was open to everyone. I watched Maggie as she jostled through the crowds of people. *She's a dentist. And she has her own dentist office.* That was really something.

"This is Nina, everyone," Maggie announced as she introduced me to Tío Max and Tía Christina, and Tío Miguel and Tía Mercedes. I met Carlos's Abuelo Frankie and Abuela Bani. I met Maggie's husband, Francisco, who was a dentist, too. I met her small boys, who were racing wildly through the house with about fifteen other children in pursuit. I tried to step aside and hold tight to my fruit punch whenever another small head bobbed past in flight.

Outside in the backyard, a group of older men were playing dominoes and drinking rum under a small tree, and their wives were trailing back and forth refilling glasses and plates of food.

One tío was talking loudly about our new president, Fernandez, and what he would do for our country. Two other men joined in the political talk, arguing that President Fernandez would help only his own kind of people and forget about the poor country folks.

These were the same debates I'd heard amongst the men sitting by our little store back home in Samana. I sat down on the stone stoop and listened happily. The heat of the sun was fading into an evening glow, the smell of garlic and other spices drifted out the doors, merengue music was playing from speakers set up in the concrete area of the yard, and people were shouting opinions about the future economy of our island across the porch and through the kitchen window. I had missed this happy confusion.

As the sun went down and the children fell quiet, the music changed to snappy salsa and older couples floated to the concrete yard to dance. They were swirling and laughing with fancy footwork I was used to seeing back home. I sang along to the music, wishing I could join the dancers.

There were teenage boys in polo shirts with white tank tops underneath. They hung around in the yard watching the dancers but they didn't seem to notice me. Carlos was circulating and talking to his family, but he introduced me to everyone and sat with me when he wasn't being dragged away to talk about his great future with one grown-up after another. That was Carlos's favorite topic anyway.

A group of teenage girls wearing T-shirt dresses in bright, bold colors began dragging the guys to the dance floor. They were laughing and flocking around the guys like a ring of colorful frosting. I glanced down at my plain white pants and flowered blouse and I wished I had worn that pink toe ring from Eva and Mirabel.

One girl threw up her hands in frustration at her partner. "You live too long in America," she said. "You don't even know how!"

Carlos drifted to the sidelines next to me. I noticed he was tapping his foot in perfect beat, and his hips were swaying to the congas of the El Gran Combo salsa.

"You know how to salsa?" I asked jokingly.

He turned around with a "who, me?" look on his face.

"Or are you just pretending?" I smiled. He was not bad looking, I thought. He had light brown skin and a crooked smile and except for some acne on his forehead, he was what Mirabel and Eva would call a young *papi chulo*. I could tell he rubbed medicine on his forehead because it was lighter toned than the rest of his face.

"I know how but I can only dance with a very good partner or else I mess up," he answered.

I nodded my head. "Yeah, I know what you mean. The better your partner, the easier it is."

"Are you any good?"

"I'm just okay." I wasn't going to tell him I danced mostly in the mirror.

"They say the best dancers always sit on the sidelines first checking out the competition."

"What?" I tried to sound indignant, but I was enjoying myself, even if I didn't feel that magical thrill like I did when Luis looked at me.

From under my lashes, I saw Carlos's hand reach out toward me. "Would you like to dance?" he asked.

Carlos's dark eyes were clear and friendly.

I took his hand. "Okay. But I'm not that good, remember."

"That's okay." He pulled me up with a smirk. "I'm fantastic."

Before I could say anything else, Carlos had spun me into a terrific salsa twirl that woke up my whole body. It had been so long since I had danced.

Carlos's style was part classic salsa, part hip and free flowing, a hybrid of dance that I loved. I had danced just like this alone at night in my bedroom in Samana listening to Marc Anthony on the radio. Now here in Neuva York I had actually found a partner.

When the first song ended, I was out of breath. People had stepped back to watch, and they were clapping for us. Carlos pulled me close to him, and this time our feet moved in tight, tiptoe movements. We were imitating each other's moves and flowing with each other, our fingertips and palms showing each other which way to go.

After three songs, I was breathless and sweaty. It seemed as if the entire party was gathered around the dance area, cheering loudly for us.

"You guys are amazing." Maggie beamed at me.

As we downed two glasses of water, Carlos and I looked at each other and burst out laughing.

"Man, you sure can dance," he said.

"And you sure can lie!"

"Who would have thought?"

"What?"

"That me, a Dominican York and you, a recent

transplant, would dance the exact same way!"

As we made our way through the crowd, people were slapping Carlos on his back and shouting, *"Feliciadades."*

"Gracias, gracias," Carlos shouted back.

"Why are they congratulating you? I asked.

Carlos looked down at me and chuckled. "Because I got the newest hottie from the island, that's why."

I felt the blood drain from my face.

"Aha!" He smiled. "You *are* looking kind of hot. Would you like a towel to wipe off some of that steam?" He fanned me with a paper towel.

I smacked Carlos on his arm. But I was having a hard time staying mad at him. "Carlos, thank you for inviting me. I love this party."

Just then another person strolled by and hugged Carlos. *"Felicadades,* man."

Carlos turned and gave me a smug smile. "Come on, let's get some cake."

I hurried after him. "Carlos, what's going on? Why is everyone congratulating you like you won some big prize?"

Carlos stopped walking and threw up his hands like I had finally broken him.

"It's my birthday!"

"It's *your* birthday?" I asked incredulously.

Carlos shook his head. "Wake up, *Nina*, this party is for me!"

"Oh!" I felt like a fool.

"Well, aren't you going to say anything else?"

"Happy birthday," I said meekly. "But you could have just told me?"

"Nah," he smiled. "It was more fun watching you sweat."

I reached up to hug him and at that moment I felt as if I had known Carlos for a very long time. *"Felicidades,"* I whispered.

He hugged me back. *"Gracias.* Now can we eat some cake?"

My first male friend, I thought as I watched Carlos pick up two paper plates with cake for us.

"So, Nina, how do you like living in Washington Heights?" he asked as we settled down on a sofa.

I stopped with my fork in midair. Right then I knew that I would never tell Carlos about life in Darrio's apartment. And so I told another lie. I told him that living there was just fine.

25

AFTER THE PARTY AND the dancing and the cake and laughter, Carlos and I got back to the subway and headed home to the Heights. My head rocked back and forth to the rhythm of the train, and my eyes were closing down so I rested my head on Carlos's shoulder. It felt comfortable and I thought wouldn't it be great if Carlos and I could go dancing all over the city and then take long train rides home afterward. At least I had something to tell Mami when Darrio and I called her. She'd be happy about this "date."

We finally arrived at our stop after 10:00 p.m. Carlos was walking me to my building when a white Jeep drove by and slowed down. I knew without looking who the driver was. Carlos must have known, too, because he began walking faster and took my hand in his protectively. The Jeep sped up and drove off but I felt so strange, as if the entire beautiful day was spoiled somehow because Luis had seen me, walking hand in hand with Carlos.

"You know who that was, right?" Carlos wasn't beating around the bush.

I nodded.

"I hope you aren't still interested in him, Nina."

"He's not so bad, Carlos. In fact, he's a pretty nice guy."

"Of course he's pretty nice. Do you think the devil would show up looking ugly and being mean to you?"

"You're calling Luis the devil?"

Carlos shook his head. "Don't waste your time, Nina. And in case I haven't made *my* intentions clear, I am very interested in going out again, okay?" And with that Carlos leaned over and kissed me on my cheek. He opened my building door for me, ushering me in.

I whispered good night and hurried toward the elevator. I had to tell Carlos soon that I didn't share his feelings, that I wanted us to be good friends but nothing more.

It seemed to me that love should feel powerful, like the magic of a tree in full bloom. The way I was starting to feel about Luis. Maybe I'd read too many love stories, but I needed to trust in myself and my choices.

26

LESS THAN A WEEK later, Luis Santana walked right into our apartment. I was home making dinner when the buzzer rang and Darrio went to answer it. But this time he was gone only a moment. He walked back in giving me a puzzled look, and Luis Santana was behind him. My hands stilled at my side. I could feel the heat of the kitchen glowing around me in iridescent colors and a Sunday school Bible quote popped into my head.

His eyes are like a flame of fire, and on his head are many royal crowns. He has a name written on him that nobody knows except himself.

I wondered what he was doing here. *Oh, please don't let*

him be one of Darrio's "customers." I continued cooking the rice and beans, chopping up cilantro and garlic as if nothing had happened. But the world was spinning fast beneath my feet. Luis watched me and eventually the steam in the hot room began to get to him. He wiped his forehead with a handkerchief he took out of his back pocket. I wondered for a second who washed and ironed his handkerchiefs into such perfect white squares.

Luis sat down with Darrio at the small table. They were talking quietly, and I couldn't hear a word of it. Darrio's face changed expressions fast, and I felt like I was watching a silent movie. Finally, they stood up.

I finished up the cooking and wiped my face. I was fanning myself with a paper fan when Luis came over to me.

"Nina, would you like to go for a drive with me?"

"Como?" I asked. "What?"

"A drive," he said again. "Far away from this hot kitchen."

I stared at him. "Is Darrio coming, too?"

"No, I'm inviting you."

What was Luis thinking? I couldn't just pick up and go with him for a drive without my brother.

Just then Darrio spoke up. He nodded his head at me.

"It's okay, Nina, Luis will take care of you."

"What about dinner?" I gestured helplessly at the food I had just cooked.

Darrio came over and patted my arm. "It's okay, *mi amor*, I'll eat it all." He smiled at Luis and me. But it seemed like a strained smile.

I glanced up at Luis from under lowered eyelashes. I was afraid to show my eyes because of the excitement I was feeling. Part of me wanted to leap up and down. The other part wanted to scream "What's going on?" But something was holding me back. I couldn't understand the look on Luis's face. I didn't know enough about men to understand the feelings I was picking up from both Luis and Darrio. It almost felt like a standoff or a battle between them, but why was Darrio letting me go?

I looked at my brother again. His expression was filled with concern, but he also looked resigned. What had Luis said to Darrio?

"I would like to go for a drive," I said, focusing on each word so they would not tremble. "I'll be right back."

I went to my room and pulled a comb through my hair. I hurriedly changed into a pretty sundress and sandals, and tied a fringed band around my hair to get it off my face. I let my hair hang down my back. I kissed Darrio good-bye on his cheek. Then I looked at Luis.

"Okay?"

Luis nodded.

We did not speak as we waited for the elevator or as we walked toward his big, white, gleaming Jeep. He opened the door for me as if I were really a princess. I climbed inside and sat on the deep, smooth leather seats and felt for the first time in my life what it must be like to be rich. The leather smelled luxurious and the gleaming wood panels on the dashboard were almost like mirrors. Luis climbed in and turned on the powerful engine, then adjusted the air conditioner all the way up so the icy coolness blew all over me. He leaned back a moment and looked at me.

I sank into the passenger seat and stared out at the hot Washington Heights world as if I were inside a glass ball.

"Te gusta?" asked Luis. "You like?"

"Yes. I like it for sitting inside on a hot day and nothing more."

"What does that mean?

"I don't like it enough to want it." I knew what gifts can cost a young girl. Mami had already made that clear to me. Luis glanced at me and raised his hand off the steering wheel to wave at someone calling to him. "How long you been in New York?"

"Almost three months," I said quickly.

He shifted the gears and pulled out. "Let me show you something."

27

AND THAT WAS THE beginning of my other life—the one built on fantasy and fairy tales, the one my mother dreamed of for me, the one where some rich, handsome prince would carry me off to live happily ever after. As if that could really happen in a world like this! I was smart enough to know the reality of my life in Washington Heights. But for one day, this one special day, I could pretend I was a princess riding with a prince in a fancy chariot, seeing the sights of a new world painted silver and gold.

As we drove away down St. Nicholas Avenue, Luis turned to me and asked, "Do you love him?"

"Who?"

"The boy I saw you with, do you love him?" I was right, it had been Luis in the Jeep that night I walked home with Carlos.

"Carlos?"

Luis's mouth looked grim. He nodded his head.

"No, not like *that*," I stressed.

"Not like that?" asked Luis, looking over at me as he drove.

"No." I shook my head. "Not at all."

Luis smiled like I had just given him a big present.

"I told Darrio about you," I added, just so he'd know I wasn't hiding anymore.

"I was planning to tell him if you didn't. I wasn't going to sit by and watch you go parading around my neighborhood with other men." Luis reached over and squeezed my hand, and I left my hand in his. He drove like that for a little while, and I marveled that this was our first date, our first everything, and I knew this day would be the best one of my life so far. I just knew it. This was the man I was supposed to be with. The heart never lied, said Señora Rivera.

Luis drove past the *colmado,* where I could see her sitting at her register, past the drug dealers leaning up on the walls, past the corner where the A train stopped, and onto the highways that twisted and turned like concrete serpents.

The air-conditioning blasted me with beautiful, cold air. I didn't speak as Luis drove past a towering bridge. The George Washington Bridge, he told me. A wide river stretched below it, and tall buildings glittered on the horizon.

We flew along a highway at the edge of the Hudson River until Luis pulled into a side street and parked. We walked to the edge of the river. It was soothing to see water again—not the deep blue of an ocean or the beautiful bay of my home, but gray water shifting beneath us like a mystery.

And then, there she was. The Statute of Liberty! She floated like a proud woman on the water, as if saying, *See, I'm here, still going strong.*

In my mind, I answered her, *Yes, I'm strong, too. Watch me.* We walked along the promenade as Luis told me the famous story of how France gave the statue as a gift to the United States. Luis bought us hot dogs and sodas at a vendor and we continued walking and eating.

"My mami and I used to do this back home," I said,

bringing up the past for the first time. "We'd walk by the water eating and chatting every week."

"Do you miss her a lot?"

I stopped walking and looked up at the hazy afternoon sky. "Yes, but not the way you'd think."

"Explain."

"Part of me is sad because I'm not with her every day doing all this things we enjoyed, and another part is sad because she doesn't understand me at all. And I see that so clearly now that I'm here."

We walked in silence for a few minutes. I was hoping Luis would share something about his own life, some information about his mother or his father. Did he have any brothers and sisters? But he never wanted to talk about his life.

"Maybe your mother thinks you don't understand her, either," said Luis.

I pondered that idea. "Probably."

Thinking about Mami and me walking along the *malecón* was making me teary eyed. I tried to wipe my eyes with my napkin and act as if it was the glare of the sun. But Luis caught on. "It's okay to be sad, you know. You can't be happy all the time."

"I feel happy *and* sad. Has that ever happened to you?"

"No." He looked mystified. "That must be a girl thing." I swatted him with my napkin.

"Does that mean you can like me and hate me simultaneously?" joked Luis.

"You never know," I teased. "We *mujeres* are known to be a bit crazy."

Luis pretended to shudder, and I cracked up. We walked back to the Jeep and continued our drive.

As we passed Macy's and the Empire State Building, I craned my neck left and right. Good thing we got stuck behind a line of yellow taxis so I had a chance to see everything. "Is this the real New York?" I asked Luis.

"There is no *real* New York, Nina, there's only this city of a million different things all thrown together, and you just whack at it like it's a piñata until it reveals what you like. There's something for everyone here, trust me."

We drove down the famous Fifth Avenue, and Luis pointed to St. Patrick's Cathedral. But I only glanced at the beautiful church. My eyes were caught by something else on the other side of the street.

"Stop, stop." I clutched at Luis's arm.

It was the most amazing thing I had ever seen. A

magnificent towering sculpture of Atlas holding the weight of the world on his shoulders. I had read about the Greek myths in English school back home, and here was one of the Titans, massive and strong, dominating the sidewalk.

I asked Luis if we could see it up close. He drove around until he found a parking space, which was not easy. Then we walked back to where I could stare at Atlas. For a flicker of a moment, I thought of Darrio. "Luis, do you see that? Do you see?" I grabbed his arm to steady myself as I tilted my head back to take in the beauty of the giant bronze sculpture. I could look at it forever! If I were home in Samana, I would sit right here and not move.

Luis stood there as I walked slowly around Atlas a few times. Finally, I stopped next to Luis again. I raised my eyebrows approvingly.

"You can walk around him one more time," Luis offered with a grin.

"Nah. That's okay. I'll just stand here and stare."

Luis squeezed my hand. "Some people see more than others. You're one of them."

"Hmm."

I wanted to twirl around right there on the sidewalk,

like a planet around a giant sun.

"Anything else?" I asked.

Luis pushed his dark hair off his forehead. "There's Rockefeller Center."

He led me through a garden of flowers with stone statutes of playful cherubs spouting water. The goldenrods nodded their heads at me and I bent down to examine the soil. "Not bad for the city," I said.

"Glad you approve."

Suddenly, I was almost blinded by another magnificent statute—this one was Prometheus stealing fire from the gods and bringing it to Earth. Who made these beautiful things? At least now I knew what people meant about the streets of New York flowing with silver and gold—these sculptures seemed to spring up from the ground like jewels.

Luis and I rode a glass elevator down into a cool marble lobby to a restaurant facing Prometheus. Luis took my hand as a young woman seated us at a small window table where I could sit and gaze up at the golden statue.

"A bit different than the hot dog vendor, huh?" Luis asked.

I looked around in complete awe. It was the fanciest

place I'd ever been. I wished Mami could see me here. Luis must have read my mind because he pulled out his cell and snapped my picture and then one of me and Prometheus through the window. "We'll get some of you outside, too."

"Thanks, I want to send them to Mami." Mami would stick them up in her store and tell everyone that her daughter was dating a rich man. I shook my head at the thought.

"This is one of my favorite places. I used to love exploring New York with my . . ." He stopped in midsentence.

"With whom?"

"Never mind."

I was dying to know what he was going to say, but I reminded myself about patience and all you can gain from it. I sipped my Coke that the waiter brought for me. Luis sat back in his seat, looking comfortable in the restaurant. His white polo shirt and dark blue khakis made him seem older than eighteen. I couldn't get over how handsome he was, either, like one of these Greek gods. His face had the same intense look of a statue.

"Luis, how did you get Darrio to change his mind about you?"

Luis looked out the window. "I didn't, not really."

"But he said it was okay for us to come on this drive together?"

Luis only nodded.

"Well, why?" I pressed. "What did you say to him?"

"I presented him with two options. When he heard what they were, he said I could take you out."

I frowned. "What were the options?"

Luis didn't answer my question. He just kept looking out the window and then he spoke. "Did you know that the gods chained Prometheus to a rock because he stole fire to give to the people?"

"Yes."

"And a giant eagle ate his liver every day. And every night the liver grew back to be eaten again."

"I know." I wondered where Luis was going with this. He looked almost tormented.

"It's a terrible punishment." He took a deep breath and let it out.

"But's it's just a story, a myth."

"There are hidden messages in myths. Clues."

This was the closest Luis had come to saying anything personal about himself.

"Sometimes even if you're doing something for a good

reason like Prometheus did, you still get punished," he said.

"So life isn't fair, is that what you're saying?"

He looked at me and gave a snort, "No, it's not."

"We were reading a play in class, and someone said I was like a unicorn in the story."

"It's because you're unique."

"But the unicorn is made of glass, and its horn breaks."

"Well then, that's not you because you're not fragile and you're not going to break."

"That's what I thought, too." I almost said that Carlos was wrong, but I kept it to myself. I sat back feeling like Luis knew me more than anyone else did.

"Anyway," I said, "you didn't answer my question. What were the options you gave Darrio?"

"Look, Nina, that's not important. What's important is that we are here right now."

He reached across the table and touched my arm. "Tell me about your orchids. Are you growing any more?"

I recognized deflection when I saw it. I figured he would tell me more when he was ready. I sketched pictures of my orchids on the napkins. I explained how I planned to grow hybrid orchids and create a new species.

As I spoke, Luis asked a lot of questions and gave me a

few suggestions, and I couldn't help but notice that his eyes changed a lot. One minute they lit up like green sparks and the next they were cloudy and confused. You could see everything he felt in his eyes. After a while, I stared out the window again at the beautiful Prometheus soaring above us.

"Poor Prometheus," I said.

"Maybe he should have left the fire where it was."

"No!" I exclaimed. "Then we would have stayed in the dark."

"Some say ignorance is bliss."

I stopped sipping my Coke and looked right at Luis. "I don't know about you, but *I* prefer to know the truth." I couldn't believe I was speaking so forcefully. "Don't you think people should know both the good *and* the bad?" I asked.

"Definitely," said Luis. Then he grinned at me. "Nina, is there something you would like to tell me about yourself? You have a deep dark secret you're hiding from me?"

"Uh, no," I answered quickly, too quickly.

He raised his eyebrows.

"What about you? Is there anything I should know about you?"

"Oh, yes, there's a whole lot you should know." He had a mysterious smile on his face.

"Are you a drug dealer?" I blurted out.

Luis almost knocked over his glass. "What?"

I felt like a fool.

"Nothing. It was dumb."

"No." Luis held up his hand. "It's not dumb. It's a question."

I slid down in my seat.

"You want to know if I'm a drug dealer?"

"Well, I believe you're not just a barber."

"So, drug dealer was what came to mind instead?" I squirmed in my chair and felt worse than before.

"No. It was a rumor I heard."

"And you came out on a date with a guy you thought might be a drug dealer?" He enunciated each word slowly, staring at me like I was insane.

I couldn't slide down any farther in my chair without hitting the floor.

I shook my head. "No. Maybe, I don't know. I'm confused."

Luis shook his head. "Yes, you are confused and, for the record, no, I am not."

"Okay," I said, relieved. I was so ready to drop this topic.

"That's not my style."

What did that mean? Not his style!

"We have to be getting back now," Luis said abruptly.

I jumped. "Why?" I must have upset him. He was paying the bill and looked anxious to leave.

As he drove back to Washington Heights, I felt I had lost a great opportunity to find out more about Luis. Why had I blurted out that stupid question? I should have asked him about himself, not made an offensive accusation.

I wanted to tell him I was sorry, but he was driving fast and ignoring me. When we got to my building, he got out, escorted me upstairs, then said good-bye quickly and left. After the beautiful afternoon we had had, I now felt deflated. I slumped off to my bedroom and lay in the dark. When I awoke, it was after eleven o'clock and the apartment was quiet. I thought about Luis. I had never had a boyfriend.

Mami would approve of Luis's car and his clothes. She would *not* wonder where Luis got the money to buy his big, white Jeep, which even I could tell was a car that was driven only by the rich, the famous, or the guilty.

I could practically hear the conversation Mami and I would have if she were here.

It doesn't matter how he bought his nice car, mi amor, she'd say.

Yes, it does, Mami. I don't want to love a criminal.

Who said anything about criminal?

Well, he could be a drug dealer, Mami, or something worse.

Just meet his family, mi amor, *I'm sure he's fine.*

That last remark would be Mami's way of saying that as long as his family was acceptable, then he was okay. Because that was how it worked back home. Sadly, Mami was not the only one who thought like that.

Mami never once asked Darrio how he earned all the money he sent us. Or where he got five thousand U.S. dollars to buy me a visa so fast. Darrio never talked about it, either. Ignorance wasn't blissful. Ignoring the truth meant accepting lies as your reality.

I felt like Prometheus chained to a rock, with pieces of my soul eaten away by deception. I knew I had the power to break the chains just by speaking up and asking Darrio about the room. But I couldn't. Not yet anyway. What would happen if I told Darrio or Mami what I knew?

28

THE NEXT DAY WAS hot and steamy, even hotter now that I knew the luxury of Luis's air-conditioned Jeep. Before noon, Darrio came back, struggling under the weight of a large box. This one had an envelope attached to it that Darrio handed me.

"*Un regalo,*" he said.

"A gift for me?" I reached for the white envelope.

I ripped open the thick, white paper and pulled out the card. There was only one word: *Enjoy!* And below it, the letter *L*.

"Is it from Luis?" I glanced nervously at the big box.

Darrio nodded.

"What is it?"

He turned the box around so I could see.

I clapped my hands over my mouth. "Oh my!"

Darrio began pulling the big contraption out of the box. It was the largest air conditioner I had ever seen.

I walked slowly over to touch the shiny, white metal of the expensive present. I fingered the dial and read the words: LOW COOL, HIGH COOL. I was prolonging my thoughts, which were swimming in the back of my head: *Why did Luis send me an air conditioner? Where did he get this kind of money?*

But what I said was, "What about the electric bill, Darrio? It's going to be too expensive. We can't accept it."

I knew that a lot of our neighbors didn't have air-conditioning because of the Con Ed bill.

"Luis is taking care of that, too. Here." Darrio shoved another envelope in my hand. It was addressed to Darrio and when I opened it there was a check made out to Con Ed signed by Luis for three months of electricity payments—July, August, and September.

"He can't do this. We can't let him pay this bill, Darrio."

Darrio looked at me as if I were crazy.

"This is a gift. You can't send it back, Nina."

I stood there for a while, my fingers locked together, watching Darrio attach the air conditioner to the window-sill in the living room.

"It's big enough to cool off the entire living room and kitchen, too," he said as he worked. "Luis said to make sure you would be cool in the kitchen."

Questions floated like neon signs over my head. *When did Darrio and Luis talk? What did they say? How did Luis earn this money?* All I had to do was grab one of those questions from the air and ask Darrio. But I hesitated.

This kind of problem never arose in Samana. Here, there were rules I knew nothing about.

It took us half an hour to get the air conditioner unit hooked up in the living room window. And then, while I shifted from one foot to another, wavering between confusion and guilt, the frosty cold air started blowing on my neck. I closed my eyes as the shivery air swept me up in a cocoon of coolness, cruised down my shirt, through my heavy black hair, and across my face.

It felt so lovely.

"Luis Santana," I whispered. "Thank you."

29

YOUR SINS WILL CATCH up with you, no matter how long it takes. And I was starting to collect sins like seashells left on a beach after high tide. Already that week I had gotten used to my wonderful new air conditioner, and any thought of sending it back had floated away on the cool breeze.

Added to that were the new clothes Mami insisted that Darrio buy me in order to be "ready" for my rich prince. It was Friday after the air conditioner gift from Luis, and Darrio told Mami about Luis and his big Jeep and his gift to me. I was surprised because I thought Darrio believed Luis was *"un hombre de la calle"*—"a man of the street."

Mami was so excited to hear of my date with this "rich" guy that her voice trembled through the phone lines.

"Is he a big *jefe*? A businessman with a lot of *dinero*?" Mami's magic word. I could practically see Mami's bright eyes.

I took the phone from Darrio. "He's a barber at Angel's Barbershop near our home. But I like him."

Mami groaned. "What about that doctor you went to a party with?"

"Carlos?"

"Yes, him, why aren't you dating him instead? I don't want you going out with a barber. In fact, let me speak to your brother."

I put Darrio back on the line, and I could hear Mami's loud voice telling him to take me shopping for clothes immediately. "You don't win the prize unless you play the game," said Mami.

I groaned and rolled my eyes at Darrio.

"Okay, Mami, I'll take the little *bruja* shopping."

"Why are you calling your sister a witch, Darrio? Make her look beautiful, please. It's an investment in her future."

When I got the phone back, I tried to tell Mami about my orchids.

"Mami, Señora Rivera loves my orchids, and she said that I can sell them. She knows people at her church who would buy them. Isn't that great?"

"Sure, it is, Nina. But please try to look your best when Darrio buys you those new clothes."

Mami wasn't interested in the flowers at all.

Later, I stood in front of my mirror. *Luis likes me just the way I am. Stop worrying about how you look.* I hoped that Darrio wasn't going to buy me tight dresses or jeans that I could barely sit down in. I didn't want to show my breasts and wear high heels. I just wanted to wear my shorts and T-shirts and scarves in my hair. I wanted to be me.

30

ST. NICHOLAS AVENUE WAS hopping with people rushing past each other as they pulled laundry carts full of dirty clothes, stopping to buy phone cards, newspapers, luggage, and food. Sidewalk vendors selling everything from sunglasses to handbags and watches made it difficult to maneuver through the Saturday crowds.

I hurried along with Darrio trying to dodge in between everything. Finally, Darrio pushed open the door of Angel's Barbershop and walked in.

"Hey, why are we stopping here?" I asked Darrio, my heart revving up at the idea of seeing Luis.

"You'll see, come on."

Every single chair had a customer in it getting a trim or a shave or haircut. But I didn't see Luis. Merengue music blared loudly as men, teenagers, and mothers with small boys sat or stood along the other wall waiting their turn, talking on cell phones, or reading the paper.

Where is Luis? And why are we here? Darrio did not sit down to wait for a barber like the others. He walked to the very back of the store and then bent down and unhooked something. A small gate opened to a flight of steep steps going down into darkness.

I didn't ask any questions, I just walked gingerly down the stairs until I got to the very bottom and I saw a thin film of light shining under a door. Darrio knocked on the door. After a few minutes, the door swung open and I walked into a room that was stacked from floor to ceiling with racks and racks of clothes.

"See, didn't I tell you to trust me? Look at all the beautiful things they have. It's half price off everything," said Darrio.

There were all kinds of clothes, some still in plastic wrap, most on hangers and all had tags that fluttered beneath the ceiling fan—tags that read GAP, OLD NAVY, BANANA REPUBLIC, and RALPH LAUREN. And I knew. I knew that this was just the same as Darrio's secret room. This clothing "store" was just like my brother's electronics "store." I stood in the center of the room. There was a gurgling sound in my stomach, and the floor began to tilt beneath my feet. I felt like I was balancing on a high beam.

"Go ahead," Darrio said. "Pick what you want."

I shook my head. "I don't need anything." My stomach was really gurgling now.

"Pick something pretty to wear. You need new clothes." But I didn't budge.

Darrio looked at the woman sitting on a stool, who was filing her nails and watching us closely at the same time.

"She's new here. She's never been shopping before," Darrio said to the woman. The woman got off her stool and walked around me looking me up and down. She started taking clothes off hangers and holding them up against me.

What if I got caught wearing these stolen clothes? Could I be arrested for being here? It was not the first time that I worried about the *guardia*, the police. I thought about them every time our doorbell rang, and Darrio went to let in a new customer.

"No, Darrio. I don't want anything here."

What I really wanted to say was, *How could you bring me here? How can you act like this is normal? What the hell is wrong with you?* But I kept my thoughts to myself and pushed at the door. I didn't care what Darrio thought. I was leaving.

Sweat dripped down my neck and my back. My shirt stuck to my breasts, and men stared at me as I walked through the barbershop.

"Nina." I heard Luis's voice above the noise. It looked like he was in the middle of cutting intricate designs onto a man's head. Luis put down his razor and walked me outside. Darrio was right behind us.

"What's going on?" Luis asked.

"She needed clothes," Darrio said.

"Man, why did you bring her here?"

"You know why." For the first time ever, I heard an edge in Darrio's voice. Darrio sounded as if he was one of the *hombres de la calle*.

No one said anything for a few minutes as one of the barbers stuck his head out.

Darrio finally spoke, and this time his voice sounded defeated. "I tried not to for a long time."

So, it was Darrio who didn't want to take me shopping all along? This was too much. "What the hell is going on?" But they both ignored me.

Luis sighed. "I'll take her shopping."

"Man, you can't do that. You know better than I do how it works."

"That don't apply to me," said Luis to Darrio. Luis turned to me, "Nina, I have the perfect store for you. It's called H&M and it's full of shorts and T-shirts and everything you need."

"A regular store?"

"Yeah. Regular." The way he said it made me know I was right about the stolen clothes. But who owned this "clothing store"? Was it Luis's? Was this how he made his money for the a/c and Jeep and restaurants?

"I'll see you later." He touched my arm before he left. For the first time since I met Luis, I pulled back. He looked stunned. "Is anyone going to tell me what's going on?" My voice quivered, but I didn't care. Enough was enough. I wanted to scream at them and throw something heavier than some broken pottery. I hated the way they were both protecting me from some "truth" that I already knew about anyway.

They were both treating me as if I was some fragile thing—as if I couldn't handle reality. It made me sick. I left them both standing on the sidewalk and I marched back up St. Nicholas Avenue to Darrio's apartment, to the fire escape, to my orchids. It was only then that I broke down crying.

31

FUNNY, IT WAS CARLOS, the one who had called me a glass unicorn, who kept me grounded. I thought it was Luis who understood me, but it was Carlos who could see the whole picture.

The day after my date with Luis, I told Carlos that I loved his friendship but I didn't want more. He didn't call me for a week and I missed our conversations. I knew if he was a true friend he'd come back when he was ready. Sure enough, he called to ask if I was still interested in going to the Catskills to see Bunny perform at a place called Bard. "Definitely," I told him.

Typical Carlos, he didn't stop there. "I'm not giving up,

Nina. I'll play the friend card for now. But things change."

"Okay," I said humbly, happy to have him back in my life. "But I like Luis, you know." I had to be clear.

"I know, don't remind me," he said sarcastically.

Bunny's dance performance in the Catskill Mountains was coming up in August. Carlos had figured out how to get there by bus. He told me I would love it because I would get to see lots of trees.

"In New York?"

"Yes, Nina, New York is much more than the city. In fact, most of New York state is countryside."

I told Carlos I would believe it when I saw it. In truth, I longed to see anything that reminded me of home again. I knew it wouldn't be the acres of coconut trees I was used to in Samana, but pines and birch trees were fine with me, too.

"If there is so much beautiful countryside why are we all stuck here in the city?"

"Because we are city folks. We don't know any better. Plus, there is nothing to do up in the country."

"Ha!" I said. "Maybe not for you."

Maybe if I liked the countryside, I would convince Darrio to move there. Why not? Why did we have to live in the city just because this was where most of our fellow Dominicanos chose to live? Like Señora Rivera said, it takes courage to change your life. But we could do it together.

As I took care of my orchids, which were now selling well through Senora Rivera, I began to formulate my plan for escaping Washington Heights. I was saving every penny of the money I made and my plans gave me hope. All I had to do was convince Darrio to move. We'd have a real garden again, and Darrio could be himself instead of this imposter he had become. I forced myself not to think of Luis. Luis was not part of my plan.

When I walked into the *colmado*, Señora Rivera greeted me with a hug. "Nina, your flowers are selling fast. I need more. Everyone at church wants an orchid now. Even the pastor wants to buy some for the pulpit."

"Really?"

Señora Rivera nodded. "No one believes you grow them on a fire escape."

I beamed at Señora Rivera's news.

"You can teach a class on city gardening at the church hall, and they'll pay you."

My smile stretched from one side of my face to the

other. "I would love to tell them how to do it. But they really want me to teach a class?"

Señora Rivera nodded. "And here," she said, handing me a big brown envelope. It was the money I'd earned from my orchids.

Wait until I told Mami. She'd never believe I could earn this much selling flowers in New York.

When I arrived back at the cash register with my goods, Señora Rivera took my hands in hers. "I am very happy for you, Nina. You followed your heart."

"But what if your heart is telling you two different things?" I asked, thinking of Darrio. And of myself, too, with Luis.

Señora Rivera shook her head against that idea. "Your heart never tells you two different things. Your mind argues with your heart and gets you confused, that's all. But the heart only knows one truth."

"But what if you don't hear it anymore?"

"That happens if you stop listening. But something always comes along and wakes it back up."

"Like what?"

"Oh, it can be anything, but if the heart is ignored for too long, it will take something big like an earthquake to wake it up again."

"Hmmm . . ." I pondered this. What would it take to shake up Darrio?

As if Señora Rivera was reading my mind, she said pointedly, "But *you* cannot wake up a person. That person must awake on his own."

I walked home slowly, thinking of Señora Rivera's words.

32

ONE NIGHT, AFTER PLANNING with Carlos for our trip upstate, I overheard a conversation between Darrio and his friends, who were playing dominoes in the living room. It was all about Luis. They were drinking Brugal Rum and 7UP and slapping dominoes down on the square table. Other than Darrio, there was also his friend, Jose, and two brothers who lived in our building, Felix and Ernesto. They came every week to hang with Darrio, so I knew their voices well.

According to Jose, Luis did not take out girls from the neighborhood. So, it was strange that he seemed to have a liking for me.

"Luis only goes out with women in Manhattan.

Fancy, club women," Jose added.

"Washington Heights is in Manhattan, you *idiota*." I heard Darrio laugh.

"No, man, that is another world completely," said Jose.

"Yeah, well, the question is, why *your* little sister? I mean, what's going on?" asked Felix.

I could imagine Darrio shrugging. "I don't know," he said. "One day, Luis comes here and asks to take her for a ride in his car. He brings her back and the next day he sends her that air conditioner. That's the whole story."

There was quiet. Each guy was probably creating his own version of the story to match the questions he had in his mind.

Then one spoke, "Maybe it was love at first sight."

No response, only the slapping of dominoes.

"Maybe she reminds him of his sister who was killed," stuttered Felix.

"What sister?" asked Darrio.

"I don't remember her name."

"Angelina," said Ernesto. "It was a long time ago when Luis was a kid. He had to be only twelve years old when it happened. She was older than him and gorgeous, man, a real beauty queen."

"Yes," said Felix. "I remember she was always floating along on her tippy toes like a dancer or something. She went to that performing arts school downtown. Anyway, one day she was walking near that *colmado* on 184th Street and she was shot. Caught in the middle of a drug war."

I sat up in bed, shocked and straining to hear more.

"So, is that why he did all that stuff and ended up in juvie?" asked Darrio.

I put my hand over my mouth to stop myself from making a sound.

"I dunno. He went kind of crazy. Some people say he shot the dude that killed his sister."

"Is that true?" Darrio's voice was harsh.

"Who knows? But he was in prison for the murder."

I thought I was going to die sitting there listening to them talk. I wanted to go in the hallway to hear clearly but I was too frozen in place. Then doubt crept in. Maybe these were just more rumors about poor Luis. And sure enough, I heard Jose say firmly, "It's not true. Luis didn't kill anybody."

I exhaled with relief.

"So, why is everyone so afraid of him?" asked Darrio. "I've been hearing about that kid like he's some kind of assassin or something. What's the deal?"

Felix laughed. "It's because he doesn't give a damn. He doesn't care. And the scariest thing on the street is a man who doesn't care if he lives or dies. That kind of man is a loose cannon, unpredictable."

"Yeah, crazy, just like I said," laughed Ernesto.

"He looks like he would hurt anyone who crossed him. You get that feeling around certain people. And I get it around Luis," said Felix.

"I do, too," I heard Darrio say. "But he's nice to Nina. He takes care of her."

"Well," said Felix, "Nina might remind him of his sister. She was around Nina's age, sixteen, when it happened."

The men changed the subject, but my mind was spinning in circles. Was this the same family Señora Rivera had talked about? The one whose mother died of cancer after her daughter was killed and her son went to prison? Was Luis that boy?

Then I heard the men talking about Luis again.

"So you're saying that Luis likes Nina as a sister?" asked Darrio.

More dominoes hit the table and echoed through the

living room. "Well, man, who knows? But it's not as if she's his type, you know what I mean. Your sister is so . . . uhm . . . quiet."

"Yeah," Darrio said. "But she's real smart, smarter than all of us."

I smiled at my brother's words and lay back down on my bed. I didn't hear any more about Luis from them that night. But my mind couldn't stop singing Luis Santana's name. *Who are you, Luis? What terrible thing happened to you?*

Then, as if I had conjured him up, the very next day Luis walked back into our apartment. I hadn't seen him for a week, ever since the clothes incident at the barbershop.

I wanted to ask Luis where he had been, but all I could do was look away so he wouldn't see that I'd missed him so much. I had spent the entire week purposely not thinking about him. Now, here he was in my tiny apartment and all I wanted to do was run over to him and put my head on his shoulder and stay like that forever. He stood at the door looking at me with that intense gaze.

Then, in an instant he was right in front of me, and I could feel his warmth. I don't know what made me do it, but I raised my arms up and put them around his neck. The week's separation from him had made me bold and I felt my feminine power, sweet and new to me. Without a doubt, I was following my heart. My fingers came into contact with the skin on the back of his neck and I stroked it with my thumbs, my arms hooked around his neck. His body tensed up, and his eyes looked like those of a panther ready to strike.

Without a word, Luis Santana swooped me up and held me close. My head fit into that space between his neck and shoulder, and I closed my eyes, inhaling my joy. I could sense something desolate about him. I opened my eyes and tilted my head to look at him, but his eyes were closed. I put my head back on his shoulder and said nothing at all.

I had never felt a man's lips touch mine, and I wondered what Luis's lips would feel like. Would they be soft or strong?

It was Luis who broke our embrace. He placed me back down on my feet, and he took a step backward. He asked me where Darrio was, and I told him I had not seen my brother all day. Darrio's absence was strange because he was usually there to answer the door whenever it buzzed. Now it was almost one o'clock in the afternoon, and the doorbell hadn't rung once.

"You don't belong here," Luis said softly.

"I want to kiss you," I whispered.

"Oh, Nina," he said, and reached out for me. His kiss tasted like nothing that I had imagined. His lips were gentle at first, then he pressed harder and I moved against his lean body and pressed myself as close as I could. I wanted to be a part of him. Luis broke the kiss and pushed me away, and I was breathing hard.

He looked at me skeptically. "You kiss anyone else, Nina?" He raised an eyebrow at me.

"You mean like Carlos?" I asked.

Luis's face darkened.

"No," I said quickly. "No one else."

"Good," said Luis. "Let's keep it that way, too. Now where is Darrio? I want to talk to him."

"I don't know. Maybe he's at his girlfriend Marla's, although he would tell me first."

Luis began calling people on his cell asking if they had seen Darrio, and I began to get worried. I heard him asking a lot of questions in a lowered voice.

"Get dressed," Luis said to me as I waited.

I nodded and hurried to my room, putting on a skirt

with a yellow T-shirt and my sandals. I checked my orchids and closed and locked the bedroom window.

Luis was still standing in the middle of the room where I'd left him.

"Did he say anything to you before he left today, Nina?"

"I never saw him. He was gone when I woke up. Is he in trouble, Luis?"

"I don't know."

"He might be," I said softly. Luis looked at me sharply, and I walked away. I couldn't tell him about my family's crime.

Luis came up behind me and put his arms around me, resting his chin on my head. "Let's get out of here, Nina. Let's go somewhere special."

My heart was torn. Part of me wanted to stay home and wait for Darrio, and the other wanted to go with Luis. I didn't have a choice, though, because Luis said, "I'm not leaving you here."

33

LUIS TOOK ME TO a place that changed my life forever. A place of colors and light and so much beauty that it was like waking up and finding that my entire Samana garden with its royal palms and calabash trees, white roses and wild purple bougainvillea had grown up overnight all around me, swaddling me in magic. I had never known anything like this existed. In Samana, I had spent many hours standing on the *malecón* watching the artists paint, but I had never been to a museum. This one was filled from top to bottom, and along every wall, with paintings and sculptures, drawings and tapestries, and murals and ceramics—the most beautiful things I'd ever seen in my life.

The Metropolitan Museum of Art. I still have the receipt from our tickets. And I still have the small metal clip that was placed on my shirt, which permitted me to roam freely from floor to floor. I have no idea how long we stayed at the Met, as Luis called it.

"Luis, look at that," I kept whispering, pointing at one beautiful work of art after another. My head swiveled from side to side as we walked around rooms of polished marble floors and high, vaulted ceilings. Every room was different. And then I stood face-to-face with a painting that made the whole world fall silent. I was utterly alone, no sound, no people, nothing but me and this beautiful picture hanging on the wall, and I felt as if I had arrived at my real destination.

I was running in wild, yellow grass, dancing around a tall, dark green tree under a sky that was swirling with blue-green white clouds. Vincent van Gogh was the artist's name. Luis told me he was a famous European artist.

"He was a genius," said Luis. "But he was also kind of . . ." He put his finger by his ear and twirled it in a circle.

"What? Crazy?" That could not be true. This man who painted this was not crazy at all.

"Well, he shot his ear off," said Luis. "And he was sent

to an insane asylum. Later, he shot himself and died."

"How do you know all this?"

"I read a lot. I used to have a lot of time to read."

"Oh." I thought of him sitting with a book in a juvenile detention center.

"Why was Vincent van Gogh confused?"

"Maybe because his art was rejected. He never sold any, actually, I think he only sold one. He was constantly borrowing money from his brother to pay for his paints and canvases, and he finally gave up."

"He did not!" I protested. "He did not give up." Was I talking about Vincent van Gogh or myself?

"Nina." Luis touched my arm and pulled me close. "Why are you crying?"

"Because it's a horrible story. Think about this man's feelings. Look at what he gave us."

"Yeah," said Luis. "Reminds you of our friend Prometheus, doesn't it? Punished for giving us something great?"

I wiped my eyes. "You're really smart, Luis. You know so much. Did you ever want to go to college?"

Luis stiffened. I turned and buried my face in his shirt. "I'm sorry, I'm just saying . . . I think you would be great at college. Better than me."

Luis chuckled and put his hand on my hair. I looked up at him under my wet eyelashes. "You should think about it. We could go together if you can wait two years." I was kidding, but suddenly I realized what I had implied: that we would be together that long.

"You know, Nina, it was Vincent van Gogh's brother who supported him while he created all of these masterpieces. If it wasn't for his brother we might not be seeing this."

I thought about the importance of a brother who believed in you. Did Darrio believe in me? Did I believe in him?

"That painting is alive," I whispered.

"Alive?" asked Luis. I realized then that Luis only knew the facts. He could not feel the painting. And yet I could feel it, but I didn't know the facts. Which way was better?

"There's no confusion there. Only clear truth." I pointed at the painting.

Luis tilted his head and tried to see what I was showing him. I walked slowly over to the painting on the wall.

"I don't know, Nina. I only see a great painting. His

technique and the use of light and his color choices and composition, all of these things together."

I suppose trying to make Luis see what I saw was impossible. We each see with our own eyes.

"What do *you* see?" Luis asked me.

I turned around. He looked young here, not a tough guy or a cool barber, just a young man who knew a lot but not necessarily the most important thing. But what *was* the most important thing? *Family? Money? Love?* I went over to Luis and took his arm in mine. "I see you."

As we wandered around the museum, I found many other pieces of art to love. But none captured my heart like that painting of a yellow field of grass with a cypress tree and a sky that was changing as Van Gogh painted it.

"That's it!" I shouted. I covered my mouth with my hand.

Luis must have thought I was crazy. "What?"

"He painted the scene as it was changing, that's why it looks like it's alive. That's the truth of it."

"Are you still talking about the Van Gogh, Nina?"

"He was painting God."

Luis looked puzzled. "He was?"

I shook my head, "Not like God from the Bible, or God from a religion. But the universe's God."

"Well, explain," said Luis, walking and holding my hand. "I'm listening."

"Only God can get it just right," I explained, recalling that I had wanted to tell an artist that exact same thing on the *malecón* once. "And for Vincent van Gogh, he looked past the scene, past the facts of the tree and the sky and the clouds, he painted the essence of it all."

"The essence of it?"

"Like with flowers. They look pretty and smell nice. But what about how their beauty makes you feel? That is their spirit or essence. It's all the same thing."

Now it was Luis's turn to ask, "How do you know all that?"

I shrugged. "I don't know."

"Must be all those flowers you plant that give you extra oxygen for your brain," Luis joked.

"So Vincent van Gogh wasn't crazy or confused. He showed us the spirit of the sky and clouds and fields so that we can see God. What do you think? Didn't he get it right?"

Luis laughed out loud. "Oh, yes, Nina. I think that Van Gogh definitely got it right."

When we got to the Egyptian rooms, Luis talked

nonstop about why the ancient Egyptians preserved their dead, and how their art related to their belief in the afterlife. My head was spinning from so much information.

"I'm never going to remember all that," I confessed.

"That's okay, I'll probably never be able to see God in a painting like you do," he replied.

"Check out the hieroglyphics." He pointed to the Egyptian writing on the huge tablets on the walls.

"Luis, they look like the designs you cut on people's heads!"

"Bingo," he said. "That's my favorite, the Eye of Horus. It's a powerful symbol to protect against evil."

"Wow, do your customers know they have hieroglyphics on their heads?"

Luis laughed. "Don't say it like that, Nina. It's legit."

We laughed and kissed and held hands. As we walked out of the museum, I turned to him and said, "I want to know more about you, Luis."

"You already know more than most people do."

"Like what?"

"Like I brought you here." He gestured to the museum behind us. "Forget the facts and see my 'God' qualities, as you put it." His eyes shimmered like the sea.

"You're absolutely right. That's what I'll do."

Luis smiled. "Besides, the facts are kind of boring."

"Yeah, right," I teased him. I let go of his hand to hold down my skirt as it blew up in the warm summer breeze, and he slipped his arm around my waist. I stiffened, feeling as if Mami was watching me outside in the daylight. Then I told myself to stop being silly. This was Luis. I leaned into him, feeling an electric tingle between his body and mine.

"Anyway, I already know that you're an artist," I said. "Those designs you carve into people's heads—that's art."

Luis's eyebrows shot up. "That's not art. That's my job."

"Your work *is* art. Instead of a canvas, you work on heads—it's real-life art. Why do you think all those folks line up for you to cut their hair?" He stared right through me as if seeing something or someone far off.

"Luis?"

He bowed his head.

"She said that, too."

"What?" I leaned in close to him.

"The same thing you said. She was right here, saying what you said."

"Who?" But I knew.

"My sister. I started cutting hair when I was ten years old and she'd tell me I was an artist. It's so weird to hear you say it, too."

He took deep breaths that didn't seem to fill his lungs. When he looked at me again his eyes were green pools of pain. I stumbled back, and he reached out to steady me.

"Time can't erase anything," he said bitterly.

I squeezed his hand hard.

Luis suddenly dropped my hand and began striding fast away from me. "Wait here."

I didn't care if my skirt blew up or my hair spun out in a black cape behind me. I stood there watching the one I loved walk away from me, taking his sadness with him.

How does it feel to lose a sister? How would I feel if I lost my brother?

I wiped my eyes fiercely. I know how it feels. I already lived through that sorrow years ago.

But for the first time I looked at it differently. Darrio had lost his sister, too. Darrio couldn't return to me unless he made it here first. And he'd had been trying his best to get back to me. He had missed me as much as or maybe more than I'd missed him.

But Mami kept asking for more. And as the years passed, Darrio must have realized he was never coming back to Samana and he gave up. Those stolen items were his personal glass menagerie—a false world. Darrio was the fragile, breakable unicorn, not me. I suddenly realized the depth of my brother's loneliness.

My eyes welled up with tears for losing so many years with Darrio, and for Luis and Angelina losing time together, too. We are our families, I realized. We are our brothers, we are our sisters, and they are us. Even if we're far apart, even if one has died, we are still joined to each other from the moment we are born. I saw Luis on the crest of the path walking toward me, and I knew that I couldn't lose Darrio again. I just couldn't.

34

IT IS SCARY HOW the best day of your life can turn into the most horrific. My worry over Darrio grew as we drove uptown.

As Luis concentrated on the traffic, I thought of how he had walked right into my arms, and we had both held on tightly. Neither of us had said a word. Luis had kissed me on my forehead, my nose, and then my mouth. He had whispered my name.

I asked if we could go find Darrio. Luis looked at his watch for what seemed like a long time and then he'd nodded his head. "Any word from him yet?" I asked as we drove.

Luis checked his phone and said there were no messages.

"Luis, I have to tell you something."

He glanced at me as he drove.

"It's about my brother, Darrio. I'm really worried."

I took a deep breath. Could I tell Luis this? I mean, could I really tell Luis that Darrio was selling stolen merchandise in a secret room in our building?

I snuck glimpses of Luis's dark hair and sharp profile in the fading light.

Luis was the guy I had dreamed about back home under the stars.

"Come on, Nina. What's the matter?"

I didn't know where to start—but suddenly, all the fears and secrets tumbled right out of me. I told him everything—the secret room, finding the key, the doorbell ringing all the time, Mami and her complaints, how she was always asking Darrio to send money, me coming to New York on a fake visa, and Mami pressuring me to find a rich guy to marry. Luis calmly nodded.

"The worst part is that Darrio doesn't even seem interested in flowers anymore."

Luis raised an eyebrow.

I cleared my throat. "I know that sounds dumb, but we

planted the most amazing garden together. And he lost our treasured painting." I knew I wasn't making sense, but I had to get it all out. I wanted Luis to know there was much more to Darrio.

Luis picked up my hand and tucked it next to his side.

Luis passed the exit for Washington Heights. He drove right past it and didn't even glance back.

"Where are we going?"

Luis seemed preoccupied. He had his earpiece in for his phone, and he was talking and seemed agitated. His eyebrows were screwed up and the look on his face was stern and serious. His eyes were a deadly pale green.

"What's wrong?"

"Nina, you can't go home right now."

"What do you mean?" Luis was not sounding normal. "What's going on?"

Luis kept driving.

"The truth is," he finally said, "something is wrong with the folks that Darrio is mixed up with. I'm not sure, but I can't take you there."

My heart started racing, and a familiar churning started in my stomach.

"Nina?"

I didn't answer. Everything seemed to be in slow motion. When it all registered, I shouted, "Luis, we have to warn Darrio!"

"I've been trying to call him, baby, but I can't reach him."

Luis was talking, and my mind was swirling with questions.

"Where are we going?"

Luis looked straight ahead and said, "As far away as I can get you."

"No!" I shouted. "You have to go back. I want to go home."

"Nina, I'm not taking you there."

"You have to. I have to warn Darrio. Something could happen to him."

Luis ignored me and kept driving. "Stop the car, Luis!"

"No."

"I can't just leave him."

Luis pressed his lips together tightly. "Absolutely not!"

I couldn't believe he was raising his voice at me.

"That's my brother. Turn around!"

Luis looked over at me. My voice was as loud as his. I

was angry and scared all at the same time.

"Why do you think I came over today?" His voice was pure steel. "It was to get you out of that apartment. I'm not taking you back there now. The cops are going to be there. Darrio's partners are in big trouble, and Darrio knows everything. I've had people looking for him all day to warn him."

I froze. But just for a second. "You took me to the museum just to get me out of the way? It wasn't even real?"

"Of course it was real, Nina."

"Luis Santana, turn this car around and take me home right now." I was shouting so loudly that people in the car next to ours looked over with scared expressions.

All I heard was the squeal of rubber as Luis swung the Jeep into the exit lane.

"Five minutes, that's it," Luis said. "We will drive over there for five minutes. But you are not going upstairs and you are not leaving my side."

"Okay," I said, breathing deeply. "Okay." I just wanted Luis to get me close to Darrio. I would figure it out.

35

AND THEN, ALL OF my family's sins caught up with us in one harrowing moment.

On that fateful day when I kissed Luis for the first time and fell in love with him in the middle of a museum, I also saw my brother in handcuffs. I saw my family's life disappear. And of all the things that I remember, the most vivid is the look in Darrio's eyes as I stood there holding on to Luis's arm, watching Darrio being led away. His look said I had deserted him. It said I had betrayed him. And I dropped Luis's arm in shame because the love that had just begun was now destroyed by regret.

Luis had lied to me. He had lied the entire time we were

in the museum talking about truth and God. Luis knew all the time that my brother was being hunted. *I should have been there. I should have made Darrio stop long ago. I should have said something when I first found that room.*

I told Luis to take me to Señora Rivera's home. It was the only place I wanted to be. My apartment was locked and barred by the police and it wasn't even ours anymore.

Señora Rivera took me in and settled me into her daughter's old bedroom. It was Señora Rivera who called Mami on her home phone and explained what had happened to Darrio. Mami demanded to speak to me, and I held the phone while she cried long distance. I refused to see Luis. He came every day but Señora Rivera did not let him in, holding the door close to her body and saying that I was not ready to see anyone. It was Señora Rivera who contacted the high school and picked up my schoolwork for me to do at home so I would not fail my classes. She even spoke to Mami about becoming my official guardian in New York so that I could stay here to finish school. No one asked me if I wanted to go back home. Even with Darrio's arrest, Mami still held to the deep belief that New York was the answer to every Dominican's prayer.

I told Señora Rivera thank you. I did not have words for all that she was doing for me.

"I knew there was something important I was supposed to do the moment I met you," said Señora Rivera.

She took care of me like a mother and I tried my best to be happy, but the weeks went by and I felt miserable. I finished summer school. I missed the trip to the Catskill Mountains to see Bunny dance. I did not talk to Bunny or Carlos but they both told Señora Rivera that they wanted to see me as soon as I felt better. I did not ask any questions about Darrio. Señora Rivera gave me updates on his case and told me he had been moved to Rikers Island jail in Queens until his trial. As for Luis, I was not sure I ever wanted to see him again.

Señora Rivera gave me meals, bought me clothes, and stroked my hair. I stayed in bed for several days straight. My birthday came and went and I said nothing. One evening after summer school had ended, I got out of bed and had dinner with Señora Rivera at her dining table. Señora Rivera tried to ask me about her orchids. I told her I was not interested in a garden anymore. My mind was numb, and I didn't care about anything. I was homesick in a different way. Not for Samana, but homesick for myself. I couldn't figure out how to get back.

That's when the letters started coming. They were from Luis. I refused to open the envelopes but I left them sitting on my dresser where Señora Rivera had placed them. I could have thrown them in the trash, but seeing them on the dresser made me feel as if I still had a tiny piece of magic near me. I tried my best to push Luis out of my mind completely, but I think that hurt more than remembering him.

Near the end of summer, Señora Rivera took me to the New York Botanical Garden in the Bronx. It was her day off from the *colmado*, and she woke me up early and made me get dressed. She held my hand as we left the apartment. I had not gone anywhere in a month. It was hard at first to adjust to the bright sunshine.

"I don't know if you think you're the one in jail, Nina," she said in a reproving voice. "But you're not."

I didn't speak much as we walked around the gardens, although I began to feel a faint stirring in my heart at the beautiful flowers. "I wonder if Darrio ever saw this," I said to Señora Rivera.

"Probably not."

"You're right." I smiled a little because what I liked

about Señora Rivera was that she always told it like it was. She would always tell me the truth.

"You think I did anything wrong?" I asked her.

We were walking through a pathway of flowering plants, and I stooped down to pat some dirt around one plant that needed it.

"The real question is do *you* think you did anything wrong, Nina?"

I stood back up. I gazed out across the lawn. "Yes."

"Well, good."

"Good? Why?"

"Because you can never learn anything if you don't get stuff wrong. If you're not making mistakes, it means you're not living."

"But now Darrio's in jail," I said glumly.

"Yes, and hopefully he will learn something from his mistakes, too."

I nodded. Señora Rivera sounded so sure of herself. "Did you ever make any big mistakes in your life?"

"Ha! I'm still making them!"

"You are?"

"Yes, I am. I keep expecting my daughter to be the kind of mother I was and that's not happening. It's a big mistake to keep expecting it, because that is why Maria doesn't want me around."

"But at least you know you're making a mistake. Can't you just stop expecting her to be like you?"

"Easier said than done. Sometimes we keep making the same mistake over and over again until we finally learn what is most important of all."

My ears perked up. "What *is* most important of all?"

Señora Rivera smiled. "That is what you must figure out, my dear."

"Well, *I* want you around me."

I knew she felt the same way about me, too. For now, that was plenty.

36

AFTER MY DAY AT the botanical garden, I got into bed under the cool sheets and tried to fall asleep. Everything that had happened in the last few months flashed through my mind like a lifetime of memories. Arriving at JFK airport. Walking into Darrio's apartment for the first time. Looking into Luis Santana's eyes. Hanging out at the *colmado* with Señora Rivera. Laughing with Bunny. Dancing salsa with Carlos. Kissing Luis. My mind stopped there. Kissing Luis. I covered my eyes with my hands trying to block Luis from my mind.

I didn't want to think about him. I couldn't! I hated him. He had made me believe in something. He made me feel that I had come here for a reason, and that being in New York was going to be okay. And now I had lost that.

The look on Darrio's face as he was being led away in handcuffs haunted me. Luis and I had pulled up in front of the building and jumped out of the Jeep. Luis had my hand firmly in his, and he wouldn't let me go running toward Darrio. But the truth was I didn't want to run toward Darrio. The flashing lights and siren noises and all those people and police officers had frightened me. I had grabbed Luis's arm, holding on tightly. Darrio had looked at me standing there with Luis like I had betrayed him. Or maybe that's just how I felt.

I turned and buried my face in my pillow.

So many kids at home had to work hard to help out their families. Me, I had such an easy life because of Darrio. What he did was wrong, but he had done it to make my life better. How could I think of kissing Luis while he was locked up?

37

I DID NOT GO outside. I did not eat much, or talk about school or even talk to Mami when she called on Señora Rivera's phone. My entire world was now my room at Señora Rivera's apartment. I could tell she was getting worried about me so I tried to talk to her at dinner and act as if everything was okay, but she knew better.

Then one night, I heard Luis talking to Señora Rivera in her living room. She had let him in, but she did not call me out of my room. I heard his voice even though I could not hear his words.

I closed my eyes. When I woke up, everything was dark. The clock's face was lit up to 2:00 a.m. I looked around at the now-familiar shadows. The wooden bed was glowing in the moonlight that streamed in through the open window. Lace curtains fluttered in a slight breeze. It was so quiet. I felt as if I was floating on the ceiling looking down at everything below. Everything was too complicated. I wished I could stay up there forever and never come down, just be a cloud in the sky. I imagined myself floating off into nothingness, evaporating with the clouds. Feeling empty and free. This must be how Laura felt surrounded by her glass animals—nothing could touch her. Not her mother, her brother, not love or despair—nothing! A breeze blew in even stronger than before and Luis's letters that were propped up on the dresser fell over. Some fell onto the floor and skittered next to my bed. I leaned over, and in the moon's light I could see his handwriting—neat and crisp and real.

Then, like glass shattering into hundreds of pieces, my soul suddenly exploded from its fragile place. I saw, in my mind's eye, all the letters that Darrio had written to me over the years—his envelopes covered with drawings of flowers and trees. He wrote every single month. Just to me. And his letters had made missing him a bit easier. And then I knew. I had the answer to my question. The most important thing of all was realizing that the world isn't perfect and that you just have to love people for the good in them . . . for who they are . . . and not get so caught up in the bad stuff. Because there'll always be some bad stuff.

My last thoughts as I drifted back to sleep was of Mami standing in her store and lifting my chin to look in my eyes. She had wanted what was best for me. In her own way. And so did Darrio. And what about Luis? I knew deep down in my soul one truth: I loved him. I loved him!

38

LUIS WALKED THROUGH MY dreams, touched my hand, and smiled at me. I woke up with a still and peaceful heart. I felt as if I were floating in the clear blue waters back home.

I heard a knocking on the front door and Señora Rivera's voice. I tiptoed down the hallway and glimpsed Luis at the door. I walked over and touched Señora Rivera's shoulder and she jumped.

"*Mi amor*, I did not know you were awake."

Luis had something in a large paper bag.

"Hello, Nina," he said as if we had just seen each other yesterday instead of a month before.

"Hello, Luis. What's that?"

"A present for you." He smiled, pulling out a purple-glazed pot that held a yellow orchid with black stripes, a rare one that I had never seen before. I felt an instant shot of excitement at its unusual beauty.

"That is gorgeous. Where did you get it?" I stepped aside to let him in.

"An orchid nursery. Can you believe there's one in Westchester? I brought it so that you could start a new garden."

My face stiffened at the memory of my trampled flowers under the policemen's feet.

"Thanks." Luis reached out his arms, but I stepped back and walked to the kitchen.

"Nina, I'm making you breakfast. You haven't eaten a thing in two days," said Señora Rivera.

I showed her the orchid. "It's beautiful. He must have gone far to get that."

"Do you mind if he stays for breakfast?"

Senora Rivera ignored my question and pushed Luis into a chair in the living room.

"Both of you need to talk while I cook," she said, wagging her finger at us.

After she left we sat there, not saying anything at all. I put the orchid down and tucked my feet up under me. I lay my head back on the chair. Usually we had so much to talk about and now nothing. I didn't even know where to start.

Luis sat in the armchair, his feet planted on the floor.

It was as if he read my mind. "I'm not going anywhere, Nina. Take as long as you want to hate me, but I'm not leaving."

"I don't hate you," I said. "I know why you did what you did."

"Do you?"

I nodded. "It had to do with your sister."

"It had nothing to do with Angelina. It had everything to do with you."

"Oh."

"The option I gave Darrio the first day I came to your apartment. You want to know what it was? I told Darrio that either he found a way to get out of that mess, or I would take you out of it myself."

"You knew back then about Darrio's secret room?"

Luis chuckled. "The only person who thought it was a 'secret' was you, Nina. Everyone knew about it. Even Señora Rivera knew."

"Really?" I was stunned.

"It's been there for years. Not the same room. But in different buildings owned by the same men. They also own the 'clothing store' that's under our barbershop. Everyone who works for them has to shop only in their 'stores.' That's why Darrio took you there. Darrio knew it was all going to blow up one day. I told him it was going to be soon and I was going to keep you safe *any way* I could. Trust me, Nina, he knew what I meant."

"But now he's in prison. And he might get deported after that."

Luis's face looked grim. "Darrio knew the consequences."

"Darrio is a great big brother," I said to myself.

"I bought you a ticket to go back home." Luis interrupted my thoughts.

I sat up abruptly.

Luis reached into his shirt pocket and pulled out an envelope. "This is your ticket, and I have your passport at my house. Señora Rivera and I are worried about you, and she thinks that maybe you would feel better if you went back home. You talk about it all the time."

"You bought me a ticket to go back home?" I could hardly believe how ironic life was. All the time I was wishing to go home and now that I actually had a ticket I didn't know how to feel. I read my name on the ticket—NINA PEREZ, JFK TO PUERTO PLATA. That's when I broke down crying. Luis pulled me onto his lap and held me as I sank into the soft cotton of his shirt. I inhaled the smell of his skin, part ocean, part powder. He rubbed my back in circles, whispering it would all be okay. Nothing had ever felt so right.

When I struggled through my tears to look up, Señora Rivera was standing in the doorway wiping her eyes, too.

Luis finally spoke. "I thought you wanted to go back home, Nina."

I shook my head. "I want to go to high school and then college and grow flowers on the fire escape and visit the Catskill Mountains and be near Darrio so he won't have to be all alone up here, even if he's in jail."

"Is that all?" asked Luis. Why was he smiling when I felt so awful?

"You know the rest." I felt suddenly shy even though I was sitting in his lap with his arms around me.

"Are you going to say it?"

I knew he was waiting for me to say that I wanted to be with him, but first I had to learn the truth of Luis Santana.

I ran my fingers along the collar of his shirt. "Luis, what is it that you do? I mean other than being a barber? How did you buy your Jeep and my air conditioner and . . ." I stopped because I couldn't think of what else.

"Señora Rivera, can you come here, please?" called Luis.

Señora Rivera hurried to our side, wiping her hands and looking worried. "What is it?"

Luis looked at her, then at me, then at her again. "Nina wants to know how I bought my Jeep and her a/c."

Señora Rivera looked confused.

"Can you tell her?"

"Oh," said Señora Rivera. She took a deep breath, then looked at Luis, who nodded at her.

"Uhm, when Luis's mother died, he was still in . . . in . . .

"I was in a detention center, Nina."

I couldn't look into his eyes as I listened to the words that might change everything for me.

"Yes, a detention center upstate," said Señora Rivera. "But his mother, bless her soul, had taken out a life insurance policy on herself when she first started working in New York. Many of us did when we opened our first

American bank accounts. I remember when I signed up years ago."

"What's that?" I asked.

"Well, when Luis's mother died, the insurance company gave me a check for a whole lot of money that I kept for him."

I looked up at Luis. "That's true?"

He nodded. "I told you it was boring."

I laughed a nervous laugh. "And you bought your fancy white Jeep with that?" I couldn't believe it.

"Yup," he said.

"But I thought you were some kind of bad boy, a *tiguerito*, everyone says so."

"Well, don't look so disappointed, Nina."

Señora Rivera snorted. "He used to be a terror. Be glad you didn't know him then. It's why everyone is still so afraid of him."

"So, you've changed?"

"Yes, Nina. When my mother died, I didn't get to go to her funeral. I didn't even get to see her when she was sick. Something happened to me. I saw everything differently."

"How?"

He shrugged. "I'm not sure. All that crazy stuff I did

just seemed dumb. It made no sense."

"So why buy a fancy car?"

He crossed his arms in front of his chest, pushing me away. His muscles rippled through his shirt. "I couldn't leave the neighborhood," he said almost defensively. "But I like to drive, to see places. And . . ." He halted. "I wanted it to be special." He stopped and took a breath. "It's all I've got, really."

The deep loneliness in his voice grabbed at my heart. "Not anymore."

Luis buried his face in my hair, and I patted his head.

"So does that mean you're not going back home?" he asked. Luis didn't even wait for my answer. He kissed me right there in Señora Rivera's living room, and I prayed she wasn't looking.

When he stopped, I knew my face was bright red.

"I love you," said Luis. "And I don't want you to leave New York."

"You love me?"

"Yes, without a doubt."

Señora Rivera cleared her throat. "That's what the man said, Nina."

"I was just checking."

Señora Rivera had her hands on her hips. "Nina, do you have anything to say?"

I looked into Luis's handsome face. It seemed strange to be so happy when things were so awful with Darrio. But that's what I felt right then and there, wonderfully happy.

"I love you, too, Luis Santana."

The light that shone in his eyes meant everything to me.

"Maybe I'll go to college with you." He trailed his long fingers up and down my arms.

I threw my arms around his neck. "You will?" I kissed him soundly and leaned back to look at him. "You can study that Egyptian stuff that you like so much."

"Yeah, the first Dominican Egyptologist."

He no longer looked like a street guy, or *un hombre de la calle*. He looked like my Luis. Señora Rivera had been right. It takes something like an earthquake to wake you up if you lose your way.

"So, I have a surprise for you. Can you please get out of those pajamas so we can eat breakfast and go?" Luis kissed my cheek. He smoothed my hair back off my face. I stared at him—forcing my mind to memorize every detail, every line of his face, so I could hold that image close to me forever.

"We have somewhere to go," he said simply, his green eyes deepening in color.

"Okay, okay." I jumped up quickly and ran to shower and dress.

"I'm starting a new life," I whispered to myself. There was a lot we had to do. But we had Señora Rivera to help guide us. And I would start a new garden with the orchid that Luis had given me. That orchid was just the beginning. I was going to create something magnificent with it. And I would help Mami. It would be different this time.

As we got into the Jeep on the first morning of my new life, I asked Luis, "So where are we going? A museum? A statue? What?"

"Rikers Island jail."

"Darrio?"

Luis nodded.

"What if he doesn't want to see us?"

"Not a chance. Darrio will see us. We're his family."

I smiled. "Yes, you're right. We are."

And we drove through the early morning light of Washington Heights to see my brother, who was changing his life, just like I was changing mine, in this world that had both welcomed us and spit us back out, that challenged and rewarded us. It was all about whom we chose to be in this wonderful but imperfect world. As for me, I was the flower girl.

> *I brought a humble orchid into my room . . .*
> *Mornings I watched it, evenings I caressed it,*
> *Examining the flower buds a number of times.*
> —*Ema Saiko (Japanese, 1787–1861)*

Acknowledgments

I AM FOREVER GRATEFUL to Jose Severino, who explored Samana and its gorgeous countryside with me, and then showed me the Dominican *Neuva* York of Washington Heights. Those memories live on here, and always in my heart.

In writing this book, I had the support of many, particularly Angelica Pulvirenti, who shared her love of growing flowers; my brother, Gerard Joseph, who demonstrates every day that perseverance in following one's dreams is the only way to happiness; and my sister, Christine Joseph, who is my biggest and dearest fan. Thanks to Geno Langeno for reading this story on Water Island and helping me discover my characters. Geno, your genius is unforgettable! A LOUD shout-out to Eva Martinez for her loyal friendship and unflinching honesty. She makes me a better person every day. Thanks, girl, for being a sister to me and a second mother to my sons. Thanks to my loving father and to my book-loving mother, who challenges me to "create new endings." She's why I am a writer.

To Eminem for his *Recovery* CD that motivated pure truth and courage; and to Evanescence's "My Immortal," for stirring up all the emotions I needed to write. Thanks to Scott McDevitt for giving me "My Immortal" and all that it represents, and to Baz Dreisinger for expanding my horizons with love and true conviction.

And most important of all, to my teenage son Brandt, who lent me his creative soul during a period of terrible writer's block. He not only wrote a key paragraph in the book to get me going again, but then played my favorite song over and over on the piano calling down divine inspiration so that I could write.

And lastly, to A. M. Jenkins, for guiding me through the dark to the other side.